Anthology
2018

COVINGTON WRITERS GROUP

COVINGTON WRITERS GROUP
ANTHOLOGY 2018

Jenny Breeden, Managing Editor
Mikey Chlanda, L. N. Passmore and Gary Reed,
Proofreading Editors

ISBN: 1-945368-06-3
ISBN-13: 978-1-945368-06-6

PUBLISHED BY COVINGTON WRITERS GROUP, INC.
IN CONJUNCTION WITH
SEAGULL PRODUCTIONS LLC
COVINGTON, KY 41014

AUTHOR RIGHTS

TABLE OF CONTENTS

ACKNOWLEDGMENTS ix

INTRODUCTION xi

**WHAT WE LEARNED
FROM THE DARKNESS** 13

ALMOST HOME 14
By Kimberly Armstrong
BEFORE THE DAWN 16
By Kimberly Armstrong
SERVED 17
By Kimberly Armstrong
BLINDSIDED 20
By Jenny Breeden
DARKNESS INTO LIGHT 21
By Jenny Breeden
ALONE IN THE DARK WITHOUT 28
MY CANDY
By Elle Mott
LESSONS FROM THE DEPTHS 31
OF THE EARTH
By L. N. Passmore
ABOLISHING SOLITARY 37
CONFINEMENT
By Alvena Stanfield
TOWER OF VOICES 40
By Alvena Stanfield

POETRY 41

FAT GIRL GOES TO THE OPERA 42
  By Kimberly Armstrong
WHAT THE MAGPIE SAID 45
  By Kimberly Armstrong
FRIDAY 48
  By Patti Kay Emerson
FUNERALS 49
  By Patti Kay Emerson
PEOPLEWEIGHT 50
  By Patti Kay Emerson
SAD MUSIC 51
  By Patti Kay Emerson
WAITING ON A BUS 52
  By Patti Kay Emerson
TO BED I SAID 53
  By Barbara Howard
SAILING 55
  By Barbara Howard
EARTH'S CITIZENS 56
  By Mirsada Kadiric
LOVE IS 57
  By Mirsada Kadiric
HEIRS OF BAST 58
  By L. N. Passmore
RURAL RUCKUS, a la LEWIS 60
CARROLL
  By L. N. Passmore
CHICAGO 62
  By D. P. Schnur

CUMBERLAND CRUMPET 63
  By D. P. Schnur
JACKSON SQUARE SUN 65
  By D. P. Schnur
PHILLY FILLY 66
  By D. P. Schnur
NIGHT SIGHTINGS 67
  By Alvena Stanfield

SHORT STORIES 69

EASTER EGG HUNT 70
  By Leslie Bush
A KNIGHT FOR ELIZABETH 93
  By Mikey Chlanda
D. B. COOPER 95
  By Mikey Chlanda
NOT SCRUFFY 103
  By Barbara Howard
AN ENTERPRISING NATURE 107
  By Brad Hudepohl
OHIO STATE SWIMMING 108
  By Brad Hudepohl
HOME: A PERSONAL ESSAY 109
  By Elle Mott
'ALMOST HEAVEN' FOR SURE 113
  By L. N. Passmore
BLUE YULE 115
  By L. N. Passmore
RED HANDED 118
  By L. N. Passmore
NOTHING ABOUT THIS WAS FAIR 120
  By Gary Reed

BETHANY HEINEY 134
    By Alvena Stanfield
A RIVER ASSAILED 159
    By Jan Werff
A BEGINNER'S GUIDE TO THE 166
MID_LIFE CRISIS
    By Jan Werff

ABOUT THE AUTHORS 181

Kimberly Armstrong ………….....…..….… 182
Jenny Breeden ………………………….... 183
Leslie Bush ………………………………..... 184
Mikey Chlanda ……………………………..... 185
Patti Kay Emerson ………………………..... 186
Barbara Howard …………………….…..….. 187
Brad Hudepohl …………………….....…….. 188
Mirsada Kadiric ……………………………..... 189
Elle Mott ……………………………………..... 190
L. N. Passmore ………………………….…..... 191
Gary Reed ……………………………………..... 192
D. P. Schnur ……………………………….....… 193
Alvena Stanfield ……………………….…..... 194
Jan Werff ………………………………….....… 195

CONTACT US 197

ACKNOWLEDGMENTS

Covington Writers Group thanks our supporters:

The Center for Great Neighborhoods (CGN) for welcoming us into their community building. Eager to partner with small creative businesses, the CGN is a catalyst for positive growth in Covington, and an exciting opportunity for our group. We meet in their board room on the first and third Saturday mornings of each month.

Roebling Point Books and Coffee on Third and Greenup Streets in Covington, for providing a friendly environment whenever we needed an additional or alternative meeting place. We further thank them for offering our books for sale, and on display in their reading rooms.

Left Bank Coffee House at 701 Greenup Street in Covington, for allowing us to use their spacious outdoor patio behind their shop when we needed an alternate place to hold our meetings. We appreciate the friendly atmosphere and the wonderful coffee.

INTRODUCTION

The Covington Writers Group marked its fifth year as an active group in 2018. Our members spent most of the year working on our own writing projects, some for this anthology and others for publication as stand-alone works. A half dozen of our members had their work published or received notifications their work had been accepted for future publication. It was another very productive year.

Our poems and stories in this edition were peer reviewed during our twice-monthly meetings to improve our writing skills. They are a diverse collection from many genres, some enriched with our members' personal memories.

This year we've added a special section which contains items exploring what can be learned from the darkness (both literally and figuratively). We also opened our anthology to members of other Northern Kentucky writers groups. A couple of authors took us up on the offer and submitted a few of their favorite pieces for publication. Overall, we think this year's anthology is another success. We hope you enjoy it.

The members of Covington Writers Group express their heartfelt thanks to our family and friends, for allowing us to spend some of our time away from them while we write, share our work at group meetings, and grow as writers. Their love and sacrifices mean the world to us as we strive for success.

WHAT WE LEARNED FROM THE DARKNESS

ALMOST HOME

By *Kimberly Armstrong*

I am in love with the sky.
Mottled white gray giving up
A clear patch of space,
To view space.
A single twinkling star.

I am in love with the way
The trees without their leaves
Seem to branch out,
Reach out further
And further still.
Because only in the reaching
Do they become more fully
Themselves.

I am in love with walking at night
Past houses,
Flickering lights, through blinds
Lowered or raised.
A few barks of a dog
A couple of streets away.
A three year old crying next door.
Somewhere unseen, unknown--
A laugh.

Every fiber of who I am
Chants breathlessly in tune
With my footfalls
And the way the trees move:

I do not want to go inside.
I want to inhabit this cool, still space
For always,
Yet this time, not alone.

This is what it feels like
To find yourself at once
So aware of love as to be
Nothing but open.

My friend says it is because
Love primes us for the universe,
The banal's inherent magic
Becomes suddenly plain.

I repeat my mantra again,
Now with an even
Deeper knowing:

I do not want to go inside.
I want to inhabit this cool, still space
For always, and next time,
Still alone!

The only company I want
Is that inside my mind
My love have a love
Of its own.

BEFORE THE DAWN

By *Kimberly Armstrong*

Tonight I am thankful
For the darkness.
Tomorrow, I will be thankful
For the darkness, as well.
But if on the next day
I am not thankful,
If on the day after that
I *cannot* be thankful,
And if
On still yet another day,
I no longer want to feel
Or even *to be* at all--
Then please,
Give me your hand.

SERVED

By *Kimberly Armstrong*

First, there is only darkness.
The hum-not-hum of a room full of people making not a sound.
I've heard this all-encompassing, pulsing noiselessness before.
On a tongue-twistingly pleasant Frisian isle.

Sea pervading your psyche telepathically,
Lest you forget in the illusion of your coziness,
That you're the one living inside her, and she,
She will be known.

In a club on the edge of this continent, on a bed with he who is
Only really an acquaintance, we play, and I close my eyes.
Things change quickly when you purposefully ignore them--
The skill in which I am apparently exceptionally gifted.

They enter when my eyes are closed,
Arrange themselves like ants gathered to watch a play -- no, a
spectacle.
Antennae perched, they draw up my chemical perfume,
Hoping to get their fill; to feed on this.

The acquaintance's voice calls out commands,
Doing its best to sound self-assured. While I ask defeated
Questions in a language not my own--How...many...fingers?
Too mortified to ask in this, the tongue of my birth.

Because that would mean admitting it, admitting everything
To myself and to the universe. Did any of us even notice:
I've slid myself with ease onto an altar
On which I am what is to be offered up.

Moans convey double entendres, crying out to any
And all who care to hear: Save me from myself.
The knowledge that this which I have always hidden,
Was seamlessly bared to all in minutes.

Eyes pierce keenly like an edge raked across my skin,
Feigning disinterest, intent upon consuming conspicuously,
Motionlessly circling, hovering, ever studying
In this menagerie of unmet greed.

Defiant, I refuse to show one speck of care.
Refuse them what they lust for most of all--
The capitulation of the sacrifice,
The offering's unabashed loss of control.

Escape, leave, hide! No, dear heart, not every wish comes true.
Now, there is only cold to jar me from my memories.
Pressure, to make me suck in one more breath.
Submission, to convince me hearts beat fast for a reason.

Nowhere left to go but falling, space-time caving in.
I am not inside here--I am floating everywhere.
I am neck and quivering jugular,
Ragged breath from hanging doll.

Where we flee when the darkness grabs hold,
Occasionally shows us what we had always dreamed.
In my safe harbor arms envelop
Rise and fall along with my chest.

Patient hands measure the pauses
When I forget to breathe,
And warm lips perch a hair's breath away,
Whispering tendernesses no one else can hear.

BLINDSIDED

By *Jenny Breeden*

Did my doctor say I have a disease
without any cure and I'll soon be blind?
This can't be happening; it's a mistake.
He read the wrong chart; he's out of his mind.

Why me? What did I do to deserve this?
How can I handle my illness alone?
To abandon me when I need you most
is so unfair. I can't face the unknown.

It's all my fault. I should have taken care
Of my health and my sight. Is it too late?
If I change now and do things differently,
maybe, just maybe, can I stay my fate?

My life is over; I cannot go on.
It's like I'm drowning in a deep, dark well
I close myself off from everyone since
No one understands my personal hell.

My reality has dramatically changed.
I use knowledge and training to fight fear,
embrace my new normal and learn to see
things by what I can touch, taste, smell and hear.

DARKNESS INTO LIGHT

By *Jenny Breeden*

While doing some research in old newspapers for a book I'm writing, a headline about an attempted suicide catches my attention. As I read through the article, I imagine how the events could have unfolded . . . had I been there, like a fly on the wall, so to speak.

***

On a warm June evening a young woman was seen standing on the edge of the Roebling Bridge. Fearing she might jump into the Ohio River, someone called the Covington Police. Officer Williams found her clinging to the stone abutment surrounded by concerned onlookers who were trying to persuade her from jumping. The officer managed to grab her and pull her to safety.

"Why would you try to kill yourself?" the officer asked her once they were safely on the ground.

"I'm so sick and tired of my life and I just wanted to die." That was all she had to say.

He transported her to the station house where she was identified as Anna Jones, who had turned eighteen earlier in the month. Officer Williams noticed the small rips in the short-sleeved flower print dress she was wearing. Bruises and welts were clearly visible on her arms and legs. Her eyes were more reddened and bloodshot than mere crying could justify.

He immediately took Anna to see Chief Randall who had received some training in psychological cases. He hoped the Chief's compassionate nature would allow Anna to feel comfortable in opening up to him. After a few minutes in his office, she began talking to him.

"For the past two years, I've been living with my older brother, John Jones, and a woman he moved into his house named Mary Parker. He calls her his wife although they were never married . . . as far as I know."

Recalling her current age and that she'd been at her brother's for two years, Randall wondered why a sixteen year old wouldn't be living at home. He asked, "Where are your parents? Are they still living?"

Anna was unwilling to answer but Randall convinced her she would feel better is she confided in him. "My mother died when I was a child," she admitted, "but my father is living on the other side of town."

"Shall I call him to come to get you?" Randall asked.

"No! Don't tell him I'm here. He's a drunkard and a mean man. I want nothing to do with him."

"Why not?" Randall reached for the telephone. "What's his number? I'm sure he'll come . . ."

"No, please! I'm begging you! Don't call him!" Anna cried.

Confused by her strange reaction, Randall asked Anna for more details.

"When my brother was old enough to work, Father threw him out of the house. Mother was gone and I was only twelve but Father said it was my responsibility to be the woman of the house. He said I had to take care of him. At first that meant cleaning the house and cooking his meals. It wasn't long before he forced to me to submit to his passions. Finally when I was sixteen, I ran away to my brother's house seeking refuge."

Randall handed Anna a glass of water. In the pause, he asked, "So then what happened?"

She gulped down half the glass before responding. "John is seven years older than me. He agreed to let me stay with him and everything seemed fine at first. But soon after moving in, he began to follow in Father's footsteps," she trembled, "and then became even worse."

"Are you saying your brother sexually abused you too?"

Anna nodded her head as she set the glass on the desk in front of her.

"Why didn't you leave his house? Wasn't there someone else you could have stayed with?"

"No one here in the city," Anna said. "About a year ago, I did meet a very nice young man who was about my age . . . just a year older than me. Richard and I became friends and then things got more serious. I didn't tell John about him because I feared what he might do to Richard.

"About four months ago, Richard had to leave for a lucrative job in Chicago. Before he left, Richard professed his love for me and we secretly got engaged. The plan was for him to get settled into his new job and find a suitable apartment for us, then he would send for me so we could be married. However, my brother said he was not going to allow me to leave his house."

"You're of age now, he cannot stop you from leaving," Randall said.

"That's what I thought too but I was wrong." Anna lowered her head, put her face in her hands and started to sob uncontrollably.

Randall handed her his handkerchief, "Now, now, my dear. Please go on. You need to tell me what happened today that caused you to attempt suicide."

Anna took it and wiped her eyes. "While John was at work, I received a letter from my fiancé asking me to come to him so we could be finally be married. I told my brother of my intention to leave and asked him for the $2 railroad fare. He became furious and refused to give me any money."

Randall knew there was more that Anna was not saying. Her explanation so far did not include anything about the welts and bruises. He pressed her for more information. Sensing her reluctance, he had to convince her that talking was her only option. "You're safe now but I cannot do anything to protect you unless you tell me the whole truth about what your brother did to you."

"I've said too much already. My brother will kill me if I say anymore."

"Then you are forcing me make a choice. I can arrest you for trespassing on private property . . . you know, the little matter of being outside the public right-of-way when you tried to jump off the bridge or I can have you committed to the sanatorium for the mentally insane." Randall paused to let those two options sink in. His concern was that Anna may believe either of them was preferable to her current predicament. He suspected the third option would not be. He continued, "My other option is to call your brother and have him come down here to get you. Since you haven't provided me with any information as to why I shouldn't call him, I think that is the best idea . . ."

"No, you mustn't call him!" she said adamantly. "I'll tell you, just do not call him, please!" Her face turned red as she admitted that her brother had forced her to prostitute herself to earn money in exchange for her shelter.

Anna confessed, "John would have Mary go with me whenever he arranged for me to meet these strange men and they paid Mary because John said he was sure I would try to keep some of the money for myself if he left me alone. In the beginning, if I wasn't ... eager enough . . . to go with the men or if they complained afterwards that I wasn't . . . amorous enough . . . during the sex for their liking, Mary would beat me.

"She said it was to . . . persuade me . . . to be more pleasing next time. When Mary told John why she had beaten me, he'd become enraged and take his own belt to me . . . adding more welts of his own. So I learned pretty quickly to pretend to go along with it.

"A few months ago, John allowed a friend of his, Joseph Smith to move into the house with us. I heard him tell Mr. Smith that the $5 he was charging each week was for the small room he slept in but it also included my . . . services . . . as he called them. During the day, I am required to do all the household chores while Mary lounges around barking orders. In the evening, Mary takes me out to meet men and collect the payments. When I get home, I must submit to my brother's or Mr. Smith's desires."

Listening to Anna's story in shock and disgust, Randall tried to remain calm. Looking at her arms and legs, he asked, "How did you get these welts and bruises?"

"When I told John I was leaving, he forbade it. He ranted about the money I still owed him because he had taken me in. He fumed about the money he would be losing out on from the men, including Mr. Smith. I mistakenly said I didn't care and that I was leaving anyway. That's when he burst into a rage and shamelessly beat me with his fists and a belt. He sent me to my room and told me to forget about ever leaving him. While he and Mary were eating dinner, I climbed out my window."

"But why suicide? Why not come here and report him?"

"I didn't think I could. I was embarrassed by what I had done but also I was afraid. John said if I went to the police, I would be arrested for prostitution and he'd never pay my bail. I would grow old in jail. I don't have any friends and no money of my own. I didn't know what else to do or where to go for help. Full of desperation and hopelessness, I decided I'd rather be dead than continue to live my horrible life."

Randall reassured Anna that she wasn't in any trouble. "You are the victim here and we do not throw victims in jail. You're safe now." To the knock on the door, Chief Randall responded, "Come in." Officer Williams opened the door and peered in. Randall said, "What is it?"

"Sorry, Chief, I didn't mean to bother you, but I wanted to let you know that Anna's brother and two others are here to see her."

Chief Randall greeted them courteously and asked them to be seated. He verified they were in fact John Jones, Mary Parker, and the friend Joseph Smith.

"Mr. Jones, what brings you and your friends here tonight?" The Chief asked.

"We heard from some neighbors that Anna had tried to jump

from the Roebling Bridge. We came to secure her release, thinking she'd been arrested for the suicide attempt."

Randall noticed the scrapes and bruises on Jones' right hand. "Tell me how you hurt your hand, Mr. Jones?"

Unaware that Anna had told him her horrific story, he made an excuse that would normally sound plausible. But the police chief knew better. The three were promptly arrested.

***

Although I can't find any follow-up articles in the newspapers to say what happened to Anna and her brother, I want to believe that everything worked out in her favor. I imagine that while John, Mary and Mr. Smith were locked up in jail that night, Anna went back home and packed her things.

She found the hiding place where John stashed all the money she had earned for him. With Richard's letter in one hand and her suitcase in the other, she headed to the train station and bought a one-way train ticket to Chicago. She sent Richard a telegram telling him she of her arrival. He met her at the station. Richard and Anna were married and lived happily ever after.

This particular story took place in June, 1892, but unfortunately I'm amazed that things like this are still happening today. For as much as things have changed over time, some things never change, not even after more than 120 years. Child sexual abuse and suicide are still evident today.

According to the "Darkness to Light" website, one in ten children will be sexually abused before their eighteenth birthday. Ninety percent of child sexual abuse victims know their abusers, with thirty percent of them being abused by family members. We need to put an end to the violence.

(https://www.d2l.org/the-issue/statistics/)

We also need to do more to identify potential suicides and prevent them. Suicide is a major public health concern. Over 40,000 people die by suicide each year in the United States; it is the 10th leading cause of death overall. Suicide is complicated and tragic but it is often preventable. Knowing the warning signs for suicide and how to get help can help save lives.
(https://www.nimh.nih.gov/health/topics/suicide-prevention/index.shtml)

Call the toll-free National Suicide Prevention Lifeline (NSPL) at 1-800-273-TALK (8255), 24 hours a day, 7 days a week. The service is available to everyone. The deaf and hard of hearing can contact the Lifeline via TTY at 1-800-799-4889. All calls are confidential. Contact social media outlets directly if you are concerned about a friend's social media updates or dial 911 in an emergency.
Learn more on the NSPL's website:
https://suicidepreventionlifeline.org/

ALONE IN THE DARK WITHOUT MY CANDY

By *Elle Mott*

Giggling over the funny dressed kid in front of us, I slowed my pace. He was a little guy and his mom held tight on to his hand. It didn't hurt me to slow down. I didn't want to trip over the hem in my costume. My best friend pulled at my arm. I followed her lead to sidestep the crowd, flying on foot to the next house. Afraid my hat could blow away, I held it tight on my head. My other hand held tight to my bag of candy.

A year earlier, we fit in this crowd of kids. This year was different. It was 1979. Cheryl and I were a little too old for trick-or-treating. It was the year we should have stayed home, or perhaps done Halloween differently. Instead, we pushed ahead as the little kids tried to keep up.

We had a lot of houses in our deep pocket. Not a hint of business or convenience stores invaded the Candalaria Heights subdivision. Sloping green lawns edged by camellia trees and rose bushes were now dark from the incoming night sky. Noble firs bordered small estates which inhabited our neighborhood.

After hitting the whole neighborhood, stuffing our bags full with candy, we arrived back at Cheryl's house. Her mom met us at the front door. Outstretching her arm to point in the direction of my house, she asked, "Can I give you a ride home?" Ice cubes in her glass clinked.

"No, thank you," I said to her mom.

"Are you sure? You really shouldn't walk home alone."

"Yes, I'm sure Claudia, I'll be fine." With other friends, I addressed their moms by "Mrs." Cheryl's mom was different. She was my best friend's mom. And she was different than other moms.

I had two reasons to decline her ride home. One was that she had been drinking cocktails again. When she drank, which was often, she'd suddenly fall asleep. I didn't want that to happen with me. And, I wanted seconds on candy from the houses between there and home.

"Okay, you be safe and Cheryl will see you tomorrow morning," her mom said, waving goodbye to me.

My walk took me past a few houses to reach the end of her street, Dogwood, then across Madrona Street, catty-corner to my street, Camellia Drive. I didn't see any other kids around. Shrieks of fun were far off in the distance. I paused at my street, reasoning I could get more candy if I took the long way home. I kept going and turned down the next street, Balsam Drive. I'd take the alley which cuts through the middle of Balsam Drive to Camellia Drive. No cars drove that alley. It was a dirt path us kids took as a shortcut. My house sat one house over from that alley.

Only as I started down Balsam Drive did I realize how late it must have been. Porch lights started to turn off, one by one. Some lights were still on and I had only a short way to go, so I proceeded, skipping houses with lights off.

Ahead, tall camellia bushes edged the next house. The night sky darkened its branches and leaves to midnight-green. I couldn't tell from where I was if it would have its porch light on or not. The last two houses had their lights off. I didn't get far when a dark force jumped out from behind one of those bushes.

It was a tall guy, much taller than my four-foot-one stature. And he seemed to wear all black in an already blackened area of the street. His hands grabbed my upper arms. He didn't say anything, but I felt his heavy breath as he wrestled my arms while I tried to wiggle out of his stronghold.

My fight to keep my pride wasn't strong enough to ward him off. He yanked the bag of candy out of my clenched grip and my butt hit the sidewalk hard as he next pushed me down. I had yelled, "Stop." He hadn't said a word in his act, nor answer me in my torrid yelling. The back of him was all I saw of him as he disappeared into the night, sprinting down the street. I cried out loud, "Stop, bring it back."

I kept screaming; a loud shrill of an unintelligible scream. He didn't bring it back and no one came to my rescue. I was alone in the dark without my candy.

***

I wish I could say I learned a valuable lesson on that Halloween night. A lesson like it's not right to be mean or to take something that doesn't belong to you. It would be many years later, well inside my twenties before learning any such lesson. When a twelve year old girl alone in the dark without my candy, all I knew was anger.

For years afterward, this anger often reared its ugly head. My anger toward that tall dark stranger wouldn't leave me, even when I didn't recognize the truth behind my hostility. Anger became resentment and resentment prodded me to behave in ways which fueled my need to get even, however misdirected. I became someone I didn't want to be. In a sense, I became that tall dark stranger.

And once I knew that; once I knew I had become someone I didn't want to be, that's when I learned something from being alone in the dark without my candy. By remembering my vulnerability and feeling mad no one rescued me when robbed of my safety on that night long ago, I was then able to feel what others felt when at the brunt of my anger. By letting myself go back in time to feel as I did when a little girl, my callousness melted away. That's when I learned my valuable lesson from being alone in the dark without my candy.

LESSONS FROM THE DEPTHS OF THE EARTH

By *L. N. Passmore*

When we're young and healthy, we don't often expect a life-altering event that plumbs the depths of our souls. Life is full of surprises, like seeing the Grand Canyon for the first time. Surprised? Having come from the ordered green suburban lawns of western Pennsylvania, I was awestruck. Not content with merely viewing this monstrous canyon from the relative safety of the rim, the group I was with actually walked to its depth, the Colorado River. None of us could have predicted the awaiting trials.

I was one of two just-graduated college students who joined a volunteer church youth group, comprised of three older adults and a bus full of teens. After having spent the summer working on the Navajo Reservation in Arizona, trekking the Grand Canyon was supposed to be a treat for all. None of us had a clue. To ignorance add a heavily inflated sense of physical prowess from having done manual labor at Chinle and Window Rock. A reckless combination.

Walking seven miles of the Kaibob Trail down to the Colorado and on to Phantom Ranch to use their picnic tables, then climbing ten miles up the Bright Angel Trail—well, that sounded just like an exotic adventure. However, the Park Service designates the difficulty of these trails as "strenuous." The change in Kaibob's elevation is 4,780 feet, Bright Angel's 4380 feet (wikipedia). The hazards: exhaustion, heat stroke, dehydration, wildlife encounters, and poisoned water. Add to those getting swept away in the Colorado River, slipping on the trail and so spraining an ankle or tumbling to your death (you get the point).

That's not all. Consider the hidden emotional and psychological effects that intensify the physical challenges. Trudging footsore trails takes one five-hundred million years back in time. This journey stirs the collective unconscious, a deep ancestral darkness that stands in stark, ironic contrast to the blazing Arizona sun. Being hot, thirsty, and just plain weary, I didn't realize the gravity of this encounter with vast nature.

***

Late August. Grand Canyon. One-hundred three degrees in the shade.

Shade? Where?

Carrying water in heavy burlap canteens, held by rope that cuts into our shoulders.

Carrying bedrolls for an overnight camp on the Bright Angel Trail.

Carrying roped bundles of food, enough for twenty-five to last three meals.

By lunchtime at the Phantom Ranch the tomato juice was hot, chips crushed, peanut butter and jelly fluid, and bread mushed.

Who cared? The ranch had toilets, running water to refill the burlap bags, and we happily devoured food in any state.

Sometime after high noon, the white hot disc of the sun blindingly visible from the banks of the Colorado River, we began the next leg of our trip. The Bright Angel Trail led to the south rim of the Canyon, the Bright Angel Lodge, and our awaiting bus. But we had tribulations to over-come.

A few in our group of wide-eyed volunteers couldn't resist the cold waters of the Colorado. Two foolhardy teens got caught and swept downstream. Thank God Phantom Ranch had phones to call park rangers. Our leader stayed behind to oversee their rescue. The rest of us, carrying food, canteens, and bedrolls, started our five mile trek to Indian Garden Campground for an overnight sleep.

As we climbed the 10% grade, refreshed but hot, worrying about the two lost kids, we tried to pay attention to the sharp-turning switchbacks. But when not agog at the titanic red canyon walls, we gawked at sheer drops into the abyss. Everyone blessed the jutting rock handholds that aided our climb. A Boy Scout in our group warned that the stacked stones along the trail signaled poisoned water. Cactus and scrub, quite appropriate to the desert, seemed the very essence of science fiction, especially to a troop of greenhorns from suburbia—way out of their comfort zone.

Later in the bone-drying afternoon heat, we found out why no one takes water for granted in the desert. Our burlap bags, while still moist, were flat out empty. We looked up at the next switchback and could only guess how much farther to our overnight camp. Then one of the guys in our cluster of hikers remembered an orange he had tucked in his knapsack the night before. Nine of us shared that one orange and chewed the rind. My tiny portion seemed like manna from Heaven. Encouraged by this simple communion, we headed to a roughhewn promised land, but our Moses was somewhere in the rear. Increasingly I felt like that "stranger in a strange land" of Exodus fame.

When we looked up from the Grand Canyon's twisting depths, where claustrophobic walls fold upon one another, the sky seemed the size of a mere postage stamp. I could block it from sight with the tip of my thumb. The radical shrinking of the heavens fractured my orientation. I tried to remember being at ground level, just the previous night, sleeping under a mass of stars.

In an effort to reorient myself, I looked down to the dusty, pebble-strewn trail at my feet. The tang of this fine powder is different from the red sands of the reservation that smell like sage-laced paprika. Grand Canyon trail dust, eons old and mixed with pulverized mule dung, has been baked into a kind of primeval snuff. The bandannas that had served so well against winds that carried stinging red sand seemed way too hot in the primeval oven.

At long last the strung-out group straggled into the campground. The late afternoon sun had already passed beyond the jagged opening between faces of the canyon walls. Shadows dripped like frosting down the sides. Midway up the Bright Angel Trail, early dusk brought respite from the heat. While sweating in that widely-touted dry heat taught us how long we could wait to use an actual toilet, we were overjoyed to find running water and restrooms.

We greeted our leader and the rescued adventurers who finally caught up with us, prayed, ate, and talked of the day. No one complained about sleeping on the ground with rocks as pillows. As I closed my eyes, I let the night calls of birds and insects lull me to sleep. Nights in the desert, especially down in the now black Canyon, get cold. A kind of shock after the triple-digit temperature of the day. More than that, I had totally lost any notion of where I was—or when. At best, I hoped to awake in the twentieth century and, though far from home, still in good old USA. But being cold and feeling lost in alien territory, I was no longer certain.

As all days have since the beginning of time, the sun also rose. Soon enough we began our last ascent. Overnight, one of our party had suffered hysterical blindness and had to be led up the switchbacks by gripping the shoulder of the person in front of her. Another had twisted an ankle and many had swollen feet. Nevertheless, we forced shoes over blisters, held up those who limped, and walked. With all trash left behind in Park provided bins, we gave thanks we had less to carry, physically.

Images from this last stage remain burned into my memory. Tourists on foot or riding mules passed us as they headed down the trail. We looked at these clean tourists as if they were mad, waved our hands, and said, "Go back. Go back." As the path got steeper and the temperature spiked to one-hundred plus, my head bowed. I became acutely aware of the footprints of the person ahead of me. My efforts focused on putting one foot down at a time in a beckoning print then pushing my knees to force the next forward thrust. One. Two. Pause and breathe. One. Two. Pause and breathe.

We began to drift apart. No big deal unless you get into trouble. One mile from the top of Bright Angel's last five miles, I hit the wall. At a curve marked by a concave rock I crumbled to the ground. As if someone had pulled the plug on a barrel, all my energy drained away.

I just did not have the strength or will to go on. Nearly insensible, I surrendered. My only thought: if this is the end, so be it.

***

Someone shook my shoulder. Lost in the twilight between not asleep and not awake, I wondered, am I dead?

I heard "Open your mouth." That made about as much sense as anything. I opened my mouth.

Someone poured sugar on my tongue and held a canteen to my lips. "Sip."

I swallowed and let melted sugar ease my parched tongue. Opening my eyes, I saw one of the young men from our group.

He smiled and repeated the process. "Someone said you were in trouble. I grabbed the sugar in my backpack. How you doin'?"

Like the desert that blooms after a rainfall, I felt life return to my body, consciousness to my brain.

"Have some more," he said.

Within minutes I could stand—and walk.

That last mile passed in a sort of heightened blur. Happy faces and welcoming arms embraced us. Taking turns, many of our group pulled me onward and upward. We reached the rim of the Grand Canyon, beaming as if we had reached the summit of Everest and not ground level. My throat was still too raw to burst into song, but my heart sang.

***

Hindsight. What a gift. If we choose to use it. While the much lauded "living in the moment" is a worthy way of life, it takes thoughtful retrospect to discover just what those moments teach us. Even if doubt, fear, struggle, and danger filled those moments, precious insights from the past offer hope for the future.

Venturing into the dark, a deeply personal yet communal

experience, taught me humility and respect of nature. Good deeds can be done in response to visible peril out of basic human kindness with no thought of some supposed heavenly reward. Being young and healthy never guarantees safety or success. One misstep, one leap into cooling waters, one failure to "read the signs" can kill. I discovered the value of the group, of having friends. Learning from one another's unique talents, sharing resources saves lives. Maybe more important, makes those lives worth living.

I experienced the truth embodied in fairy tales and scripture. When all hope seemed lost, someone came along and helped me. Slogging through the heat within the depths of the earth profoundly changed my inner world, and thus my life. The kindness and help of others on my journey enabled me to trust that in future dark places I would come into the light.

ABOLISHING SOLITARY CONFINEMENT

By *Alvena Stanfield*

Reprinted with permission from "The Power of 'Yes,'" *Chicken Soup for the Soul*. August 2018.

"I can't go camping anymore." That thought came to me a few weeks after my husband's death. After all, setting up camp and traveling alone was now terrifying. So was dining out. Even attending Sunday services became challenging. The seat alongside me was now vacant, VACANT EVERYWHERE. Miserable, I spent my time alone.

The Friday before Memorial Day I watched my neighbors pull their camper down our street and wished I was headed for a campground too. Throughout the summer our Kentucky campgrounds have scheduled activities. Scheduled for couples and kids, that is. Family swim, Relay race, Treasure hunt, Volleyball, and Square dance are designed for couples with children. Here I was instead, kids grown and alone.

That Memorial Day I sulked, imagining the laughter, campfire smell, nightly insect music and occasional amateur guitarist accompanied by a nearby off-key chorus.

However, like a person who tried a plummeting bungee, next morning I sprang upward and launched a new me.

"Whenever I think 'I can't. I'm alone,' I'll do it, even if I don't want to."

I headed to the AAA office and bought a new Rand McNally Atlas. Lunch at O'Charley's had been our fav (free pie on Wednesdays).

"Parking the car?" our usual waitress said, expecting my husband to arrive. I shook my head. No doubt my expression did my explaining. She scurried away. But she returned with two glasses of water. Two glasses! Resisting the urge to race to my car, deep breaths steadied me. Instead of my usual selection I scanned the menu and ordered at random. While I waited for my mystery lunch I studied the maps and highlighted places we'd been.

"Planning a vacation?" the server asked as she waited for me to move the atlas and make room for the plate she held.

I had no answer. A chill set in, me alone? The what-ifs began: truck repairs, robbery, lost ID, prescriptions, getting lost in unfamiliar areas. But by the time I'd finished my key lime pie I had overcome my resistance and knew my answer.

"Yes. I'm going camping." Alone. To a place I've never been. That decision caused tummy butterflies. Snail-paced I returned to the AAA office and with trembling hands bought a Woodall New England Camping Guide. Since I'd never visited my mother's birthplace, Vermont, I asked the clerk to prepare a TripTik and mail it to me. When it arrived the package included a list of additional Guides and Tour Books I might get from their offices to visit interesting sites along the way.

Hmmm. Frank Lloyd Wright's "Falling Water" home, Revolutionary battlefields, the Houdini Museum, Boston's Red Sox, the Crayola Factory, New England Candle Factory, Lake Champlain, the Kazoo Factory all drew me forward out of the solitary confinement I'd imposed on myself.

Against the advice of my grown children and my neighbors I loaded my (husband's) truck and headed northeast. Did I get lost? Yes. Did the truck burn out a headlight? Yes. Did families of campers stare at me, old and alone? Yes. Did I wonder how crazy this idea was and be tempted to drive straight back home? Yes. Did I enjoy the train ride from Providence, RI to Wrigley Field? Red Sox game, won in extra innings 13 to 12? Yes. Did I nearly miss the last train to my car? Yes. Was I amazed at the enormity of Lake Champlain and the ships on the St. Laurence Seaway? Yes. Would I do it again? Do I still face fears? Yes and more.

I now attend college (free tuition over 65) and hold my own with students forty years my junior. I visit my out-of-state friends. I tutor math and reading. Eating dinner alone at home or at a restaurant feels normal.

Do I still have to take a deep breath, lift my chin and remind myself: "You can do it?"

Yes.

TOWER OF VOICES

By *Alvena Stanfield*

Driving to EWR she remembered
her departure time and flight number
eight and ninety-three arrive SFO after eleven
checked her ticket, flight insurance, snacks
filled the overhead compartment
slid her briefcase under her seat
comfortable with only 36 others on board
four villains among them
trained by a U.S. flight school
four crew members, one instructing emergency rules
breaking rules hijackers threaten passengers and crew
pilot surprised as one coward attacks, kills
replaces pilot and changes flight plan
passengers phone home hopeful and scared
learning of Pentagon, Towers One and Two
smelling death either way a few heroes conspire, united
and without "ready, set, go" or "Geranimo"
take steps to limit others' losses
near a mine named Diamond T
near a town named Shanksville
they felled United Flight 93
where few saw but all benefited from
those who chose how to die
and those who didn't
their remaining comments only recorded messages
voices memorialized by forty whispering wind chimes
near electric generating windmills
and a wall, joining other U.S. tragic walls
of voices silenced for aesthetics, patriotism
while the voices at home long for those
who never reached the Golden Gate Bridge

POETRY

FAT GIRL GOES TO THE OPERA

By *Kimberly Armstrong*

Fat girls go to the opera
Throw on their skirts and dresses
Appear in all their formal,
Goth,
And casual regalia
To both see and be seen in turn.

Fat girls walk through intersections
Eyes starry and opera-filled
While a taxi driver goes slow
  Slow
    Slow
       Alongside
Until the happy happenstance
Of an innocently parked car
Forces him to move on.
Fat girl laughs walking strong.

How could a fat girl in a pink $8 t-shirt
From Target
That her mama bought her
And a black maxi skirt floating
Just above the ground
Be suddenly so very interesting
To so many people, she wonders?
Still it exists,
And that is a sight to see,
Her being *seen*.

How surprised it is to learn
In this day and age,
A perfectly normal looking woman
Sang in an opera
Across the pond in the UK--
Yet almost none of the reviewers
Praised this woman's singing.
For one reason only--
Because this was chubby.

I went straight to look up
What on earth this woman
Must have looked like
That these reviewers
Thought they could
Get away with this.
To my jaw-dropping surprise,
This woman looked
Absolutely perfectly normal.

Statistically normal to the point
Where I would notice nothing special
If she passed me on the street.
But in the world of opera now
Beholden to the cult of thinness
Like almost every other
Facet of life we interact with,
A normal woman must have seemed
A rare creature indeed.
Especially to the almost all-male eyes
Writing those vaunted reviews.
Notably, the only critic
Who commented
On the woman's singing instead of

Denigrating her appearance
Was herself a woman, too.

Fat girls go to the opera
To both see and be seen
And occasionally, if you look closely
You may indeed notice a fat girl
Going to the opera
To actually sing!
Gamine,
Self-assured,
She may throw open her arms
And embrace the world
Boldy saying *look at me!*

We are here.
We are dressing up.
We are walking tall,
Standing strong,
Strutting our stuff.

We refuse to disappear ourselves
Into ourselves
To make you comfortable.
We take up space
That is ours,
Unabashedly.

All this soft warm delicious space
Is ours to strut and love and give.
We are not ashamed to know
Our power
Lies in knowing
Our inherent worth.

WHAT THE MAGPIE SAID

By *Kimberly Armstrong*

A magpie once told me that she
Did not want to be in love with a person.
She wanted the love of her life to be an idea.
Self-assured and determined,
At first I thought perhaps the magpie
Is privy to some hidden wisdom I am not.

There is danger, I could see, in the heart
Grabbing hold of an idea with such tenacity.
What if one spent her whole life so duly wedded,
Only to discover with shock later this year
Or perhaps this century,
That idea's abject falsity?

Would the time be seen as wasted,
The loving pitifully misguided? As though
The outcome must be known before the ending,
To justify the possibility of being wrong to begin with.
Can we plead irreconcilable differences if only one of us is corporeal?
Maybe shield ourselves from embarrassment and failure
With a pre-nuptial agreement?

To be in love idea implies a certain freedom of mind
That being wedded, frankly, does not.
A more delicious form of capture I could not imagine:
Passionate tremblings of both spirit *and* service.
Exulting in devotion's phraseology: Prayers that would
Vivify the crux of my being, as they do
All love and freedom's wayward progeny.

Will the magpie recognize her intended in an instant
Like kismet? Or will time and experience show her
Which particular idea will satisfy her wishes?
To roam in her love's wildernesses,
As well as the wildernesses of her own love.
Explore their combined heights; plumb their fault lines, too.
Seems not much different from loving a person, I am sure.

If I gave equal consideration to the meaning of my ideas
As I have my human beings, perhaps I might see that
Ideas have come and gone--a few were cast out,
Others left to wither untended like leaves in the fall.
But what about those ideas who have withstood
The test of time, who've managed to both stay
And stay loved by my ever-churning mind?

I have held them, nurtured and neglected them in turn.
Utilized them as my rock from which to roam,
Secure in knowing I had a home no matter my time gone.
I have raged at them inside my mind
For not being enough. For being *so incredibly much*
As to yield righteous, elegiac indignation
That too few also recognize their worth.

The Eurasian magpie is one of few non-mammals
Smart enough to pass the mirror test,
To possess a form of intelligence that lets her
Recognize her own reflection. Maybe our magpie
Is so smart because she always knew herself?
And saw herself enough inside her shell
To put her values into practice.

If I were to regard the ideas that sustain my world
As I do the people I have deeply loved,
I would look on them with the knowledgeable regard
No doubt our magpie does. Fascination of mind,
A friend with whom to weather the storm, a fount of songs
The spirit sings. These are what our magpie showed me
Beloved ideas can surely bring.

FRIDAY

By *Patti Kay Emerson*

Friday may be happy for some
It is the last day
They work until Monday
For others,
Friday may be sad
For the same reason.

However, for some
Friday is the first
Day of work.
Because they
Only work on weekends.

These people
Have mixed feelings
About Friday:
Sad because they can't
Go out for fun
Like others do,
But happy they are making money.

FUNERALS

By *Patti Kay Emerson*

I am so tired of funerals.
Why do they have to be so sad?
Because we have lost someone we love
They do not have to be sad
But they usually are.
I have lost so many
Friends and family
That I have been to
Too many funerals
I have been to a couple
That weren't so sad,
Because they celebrated the person's life
Instead of mourning the death
But most of them have been sad
And that is why
I am so tired of funerals.

PEOPLEWEIGHTS

By *Patti Kay Emerson*

My best friend is a peopleweight.
She is not human,
But a gray tabby furball
With four legs and a tail.
When she wants to rest
She curls up in my lap
And makes sure I cannot get up.
She has a mind of her own
And does not care what I say or do.
Her favorite thing
Is to lie on my stomach at night
So that I cannot turn over
To my favorite sleeping position
Which is on my side.
Therefore, I call her a peopleweight
Because she keeps people from moving
As paperweights do for paper.

SAD MUSIC

By *Patti Kay Emerson*

I am listening now to some sad music.
The songs are gloomy
But they are comforting to me
In my time of grief.
How sorrowful music
Can be so comforting
I do not know
But these depressing songs
Do bring joy to me
When I listen closely to the lyrics
And know they are meant to
Help us understand the artists' emotions.
I'm thinking now of my many loved ones
Who are in Heaven
And the sad music
Helps me to realize
How happy they are
And they are thinking of me too
As I listen to this distressing music.

WAITING ON A BUS

By *Patti Kay Emerson*

Oh no! Here I am
Once again, waiting for a bus.
Another hour, I have to wait.
I want to go home
But I cannot
Because it is Saturday
And the buses don't come
As often as they do
Through the week.
But thank God it is not Sunday
When the buses are so far apart,
It would be quicker to walk if I did not live so far away.
If only I had left
A couple hours earlier
I would not have to wait
Quite so long
And I would be home now
Instead of writing about
Waiting for the bus
Just to kill time.

TO BED I SAY

By *Barbara Howard*

I have a hangnail on my thumb.
It rubs against the sheets.
Until you cut this hangnail off,
I will not get to sleep.

I take the clippers from my girl,
And cut her cares away.
Kiss a kiss upon her brow.
Go to bed I say.

There's one thing I forgot to tell you.
It will not wait till day.
It's very important, I swear it is.
Go to bed I say.

I am so thirsty, I must have
A little cup of drink.
A sip of water to stop my thirst,
Then to sleep, I think.

A taste of water only.
Enough to wet her lips.
Now please go up, away from me.
And go to bed I say.

I hear a noise, a little noise,
A-knocking on my wall.
I need a light, a great big light,
To brighten up this hall.

I show my girls no thing is near,
That'll bring them in harm's way.
And with a shush, I shush their fears.
Then, go to bed I say.

My room is cold. My room is hot.
I cannot get to sleep.
My tummy hurts, my eyes won't shut.
I need to use the pot.

Will you come in and talk to me?
Or simply hold my hand?
I am so lonely and alone.
Go to bed I say.

At long, long last it's quiet.
My little girls asleep.
It's time for all good folks to rest.
Off to bed I say.

SAILING

By *Barbara Howard*

A sunny day with sky of blue.
The water's bright. It's windy too.
A perfect day filled with grace.
Love the heat and wind in my face.

I cast the bonds of dockage aside.
Sailing off for an afternoon ride.
Raise the main and trim the sail.
Snugging jib to the leeward rail.

The river is narrow, but in my mind
I slip away from this slender confine.
Travelling off to a far blue sea.
Where waves wave on, forever free.

And water knows no bounds of land.
No distant shore, no beach of sand.
Sailing up, over, each curl and crest.
Trimming the rigging to its very best.

As day is done I end this rhyme.
Returning to a land-locked time.
But my mind still lingers.
Oh mind! What would it be, to be
Forever sailing.

This poem was written and dedicated to
Ben (my husband) with love, 9/18/88

EARTH'S CITIZENS

By *Mirsada Kadiric*

How did it all start?
Where did we come from?
Why are we here?
One thing's for sure, there were no borders then.

Borders are man-made.
Our history is full of turmoil.
Emperors, conquerors, and tyrants alike.
Yet, all admired at one point.

But have you ever met a fellow human,
One who didn't bleed red?
One who wasn't sad?
So what really makes us different?

Millions of years of change,
One generation to the next,
And the only thing that remains,
Is that we're all the same.

One planet,
One species,
One life to live,
In our home, the Earth.

LOVE IS

By *Mirsada Kadiric*

Love is raw,
Love is angry,
Love is loud,
Love cuts like a butcher knife.

Love is tender,
Love is sweet,
Love is calm,
Love heals the most painful wound.

Love is harsh,
Love is rude,
Love is rough,
Love slams the door in your face.

Love is gentle,
Love is polite,
Love is caring,
Love lets you in when no one else will.

Love is balance, life, freedom –
Nothing less, nothing more.
Love has no ego, agenda, timeframe –
It perseveres, it is the ultimate.

HEIRS OF BAST

By *L. N. Passmore*

Shadows stalk the moon.
In silver cages
Cats begin to stir, stretching
Their serpentine backs.

The grass breaks free
Of its mud tomb. Cats purr.
Soon they will leap
Through emerald blades.

Along the river bank
A thousand cats whip their tails,
Making waves until
Swinging bridges hum.

With all hope lost,
Cleopatra embraces an asp.
The sharp-eyed cat
Steals her last breath.

In the dark heart of night,
Burdened with gold sarcophagi,
River barges navigate the Nile.
The cats bare their claws.

The long-lost barque rises,
Creaks under the sun's glare.
Shredded sails flutter while
The cat's bones dance.

For thirty lovelorn nights
Golden arrows pierce Amaryllis' heart.
The cat's spiked red tongue
Licks her chops, waiting.

Infinity seduces mortals
Into the void.
Cats grin. They know
The Star Gate's secret.

Amaryllis. Greek maiden in love with shepherd Alteo
Barque. Sailing ship with three masts. Literary, a boat
Bast. Egyptian Cat Goddess

RURAL RUCKUS,
a la LEWIS CARROLL*

By *L. N. Passmore*

Thump, bump, rumble-rustle-whack!
  What's that?
Crash, smash, tumble, rustle-clang-clang!
  I know I heard something!
  Under the sink? Bathroom or kitchen?
  Wild critter fiends? Scratching an itching?
  Could it be a Jabberwock under the deck?
Called Animal Control—No, they don't handle wild whackers, just cats and dogs.
  A slithy tove in the window well?
Called Police Dispatch—No, they don't handle animals A-Tol!
  A borogove up the chimney?
Called Fish and Wildlife—No, has to be wildlife—woods and streams.
  Maybe a frumious Bandersnatch?
Called Out of Control Wildlife—No answer.
  Ah, perhaps a mome rath clawing the bricks?
Finally found Gone For Good Critter Control. No, don't really kill, just relocate—at a price.
  "Great, just get rid of the noise, sounds like a manxome foe to me.
  How 'bout a relocate to the Tumtum trees in the tulgey wood?"
    " . . . Uh, what's that about the 'clang-clang'?
    Inside, outside, upside, downside?"
  "Right! Downstairs, upstairs, pipes a banging and a clanging."
"Then you might got you a Jubjub bird,
Come down from the attic between the walls!"
  "Oh, No! Second thought, no, mostly the rustle-bustle's under the deck."

"Well then . . . could be you only got you some mating
woodchucks. . . .
    I'd leave them be if I was you."
    Just Great! Groundhogs in heat.
    And not a vorpal sword in sight.

* "Jabberwocky," Lewis Carroll, as found in Through the Looking
Glass and What Alice Found There, publ. 1871.

CHICAGO

By *Dale Schnur*

Forget the big shoulders
the city that slaughters,
that builds, that sells.

The snow this morning
perches on branches and
shrubs like flocking on a Christmas tree.

Confetti white and whipped
and falling beneath the window
of the rattling El as we ease toward the Loop.

Everything looks serene and sincere
bright and clean, not tough no
threatening, nor dying under footfall.
The train rolls close to tenements
products of times gone by
but almost fresh in this first month of the year.

No one sees faces in those windows
though we know they are there
behind the curtains in the next room.

On Dearborn wind driven snow
turned mustaches to ice
and sidewalk to rink.

In Chicago it snows on mourners and
celebrants alike. I am given to celebrations
so there is hope.

CUMBERLAND CRUMPET

By *Dale Schnur*

Thursday

The morning of love had turned
to an afternoon of civil disagreement.

They then went gently into the evening
of dining, soft wine, and even softer, tender love.

She did up her hair and nothing else.
Their argument rose and fell with lovemaking
and finally died with early morning sleep.

They had promised to purchase jasmine
Blossoms and perfume, and to make the morning last.

Friday

Breakfast fared well.
A Tennessee repast – biscuits, jam, chicory laced coffee.

Her prosecutorial attitude was
Undermined by his honest ministrations.

Late day insults produced hard-edged
Epithets and words not to be recalled:
bitch, asshole, cunt, imbecile.

They sidled up to that fine line
Between love and hate, until the
Rubicon was finally crossed.

Heavy, angry, snorting breathing gave way
To a back-to-stomach safety sleep
That wrapped them in each other.
They were taken from themselves.

Saturday

He liked the bed unmade.
It smelled like each of them in turn,
and each of them together.

She laughed as he sniffed the sheets, the
pillow cases, redolent of her essence.

They lived in worlds the other would
never know. Separated by miles, states,
responsibilities, ambitions.

He knew he would never be so rich or
influential to excite her with just himself.

Temporary clawing, grasping, savage love
would never stay utopia from becoming dystopia.

At parting he murmured and impromptu observation:
Cute Little Crumpet.

Instantly recoiling, he awaited her backlash.
He knew she would feel diminution, and dismissal.

A crinkly, crooked smile gave way to a contralto laugh.
She like it!

JACKSON SQUARE SUN

By *Dale Schnur*

Now a visitor under the early winter sky
with the sun hanging low on a cool day,
I march from the French Market Café,
bits of beignet on my lips and café au
lait taste in my mouth.
Jackson Square is busy yet somehow
not inviting for the single man.

Now a traveler moving cautiously around
groups gaggling amid mimes, jugglers and
street artists.
I walk purposely up St. Ann, only to justify
a thousand streets walked end to end.
Distant jazz greets me as I turn onto Bourbon
and head toward Galatoire's.

Now a stranger queuing up on the sidewalk
and searching for a familiar face.
Always alone at home or in a crowd
I am on my private cloud in a world
few can understand or care about.
Like Pere Noel at this festive time
nothing to do save offer love.

PHILLY FILLY

By *Dale Schnur*

One turns a corner and things change.
from Chestnut onto 33rd and the sunlight disappears.
Like smiles changing to frowns
and day changing into nighttime.
And love fading to whatever it was before.

Let it go.
It is a kind of something
we don't know much about,
like Franklin's kite or magic.
Forget good times, they make your heart ache.

I've pictured your face through the years,
through the city, across the country.
I can draw your mouth, your nose, your smile
so you're more what I wanted you to be
than what you really were.

I order a pretzel at the Palestra
and barely sip a cold coke.
The game goes on hardly noticed
and between the evening and the morning
I draw your face a little fainter each day.

NIGHT SIGHTINGS

By *Alvena Stanfield*

Sometime near midnight we tied flashlights to our hats,
A myriad of spotlights
Mimicking the myth of aliens

We silenced our laughter, stilled by our treacherous plan
With cover of darkness we crept down stairs,
And outside without sound of feet or voice

Illuminating we roamed yard to yard
Rising and dipping, bobbing and weaving
Hoping to startle sleepy watchers

Porch lights flashed, and with a rush
Extinguished our globes and
Slithered away to home.

We, barely concealing our mirth
Quizzed classmates next day,
"Did you see aliens visit last night?"

"Inspecting us while we slept?"
Their wide-eyed nods
Spurring us onward

SHORT STORIES

EASTER EGG HUNT

By *Leslie Bush*

If a cockatrice is the result of an egg laid by a cock and hatched by a toad, what then is the issue of the chocolate egg laid by the Easter Bunny and hatched by a Kel?

1

The scratching and scrambling, as if some rodent was trying to dig its way into my domain, drew me from my studies. A chill ran down my spine at the thought of gnawing teeth and ripping claws. If my warding spells had not been so good, I would have felt more than a mere chill. I was a lich, an undead, walking skeleton wizard. Through the magic I controlled, I was able to animate my own dead body. A being such as myself should not be subjugated to such a trivial fear, but I was who I was. I had never been the same since the rats ate me alive. Although I had taken precautions against nuisances of this sort, the noise at the door drew my attention. It had to be something that paid no mind to instinct or common sense. Sitting back in my chair, I folded my hands on my lap and awaited the fireworks. The scratching noise ended with a pop, a crash, and a fair explosion.

"Wow! That was a good one, Mal! If I didn't know you, I would say you really didn't like being disturbed!" announced Nikodemus, the small pixie-dark elf master of the tower, as he waved the smoke out of his face.

I curled my bone fingers into a fist. "My name is Malhavoc! Not Mal! You should not speak to me with such familiarity!"

"So you've told me before, but Malhavoc is such a mouthful."

"Go away!"

He just stood there with that bloody, asinine grin on his face.

Throwing up my hand, "Why do I bother to weave such intrinsic wards and traps just for you to break them and enter here anyway?"

"Don't know, but they sure are fun to unravel."

Muttering, I calmed myself. Pulling myself back into my chair, I sat in the darkness like a spider waiting for its prey. "You do know it is death or worse to intrude upon a lich's privacy, yes?"

"And what do you have to be private about? You are a mere skeleton wizard. You have no private parts to be private about."

Without hesitation, I threw a deadly blast of magic at him. Laughing, he easily danced away. The brick and the mortar behind him shattered and crumbled to the floor into a molten heap.

"That was a good one, my dear, dead friend. Your magical knowledge is getting better, but you are going to have to work on your speed and your aim," he said. With a snap of his fingers, he cast the spell that cleaned up and repaired the damage.

Grinding my teeth, I felt the joints in my shoulder tense. No undead being should have to put up with this aggravation. The Bloody Abyss! I died and brought myself back from the Dead! That alone should strike fear into others! Unfortunately, this little maggot of a wizard did not understand that. Even worse, he was more powerful than me. One could never guess that from his childlike appearance and clownish mannerism. He wore ragged short pants and a shirt that sported an overly happy rodent, which made me nervous just looking at it. Such appearances were not becoming of a wizard of his station.

"I am not dear nor your friend!" I complained, as I turned my back on him in an effort to return to my work.

"But, Mal!" he exclaimed, as he jumped in my lap and grabbed my shoulders. "You have to help me!"

No one touched a lich! To touch a lich meant death! Did this fool not know this? Of course, it was a power that I controlled, and I did not use it here for several reasons. The main reason was that I had the tendency to dissolve any organic matter I touched. I needed to touch the pens and books that I used. I had tried keeping my grimoires by magic before, but the results were not to my liking. After all, my handwriting was hard enough to read without trying to decipher it from a third party scrawl. I also gleaned more of the intent of the writer from the books if I came physically in contact with them. Because of this, I did not have this spell invoked, and I allowed the master of the tower to survive this encounter.

Looking calmly into those dark, almond-shaped eyes, I said, "You do know that I can pull your still beating heart out of your chest?"

"That could be fun! I would like to see what my insides look like, but later, my bony friend. This is an emergency!" he told me as he jumped from my lap.

Crossing my arms, I caused the fires of my eyes to burn fiercer. "Is this another emergency like that time you pulled me into that dimension, forced an empty bag into my hands, and took me house-to-house to beg for candy?"

"Hey! You got quite a haul that night!"

"I am not a beggar! I have never been a beggar! I despise beggars!" I protested, as I stood up to tower over him.

"Yeah, Yeah. It was Halloween, and it's expected of spooks like you to be paid a tribute."

"I want nothing to do with anything that is hallowed, and I really do not understand what candy has to do with it all," I replied, as I sunk back down into my chair.

"You think too much."

"I DO NOT EAT!"

"Yeah, but Tallon and I enjoyed your sack full of candy. We'll have to do that again!"

"I will be a pile of dust before I allow you to do that to me again!" I turned my back on him, but he remained in the middle of my room, whistling a dirty song that, unfortunately, I knew the words to. I threw down my pen and turned on him. Lords of the Abyss, I would never get anything done with him around! "Alright! What is this emergency you have?"

"The chocolate egg that the Easter Bunny gave me is missing!"

"Who or what is this Easter Bunny, or do I dare ask?"

"The Easter Bunny!" he exclaimed, as he spread his arms wide. "He is the most fantastical fantastic beast to ever walk . . . well, hop, … through his dimension."

"Does this being rank up there in absurdity like that Santa Claus person? If so, I will stay here. My studies are much more important."

"Ah, come on, Mal. This is an extraplanar being of extraordinary power. That in and of itself should tweak your interest, and he gives out candy!"

"What is so great about this candy?"

"You don't have a tongue, so you miss out on the exquisite pleasure involved with such things, especially chocolate."

"I prefer to keep it that way."

"Come. Help me look for it."

Crossing my arms again, "Why would I help you find your lost candy? What is in it for me?"

"I'll split it with you!" he answered enthusiastically.

"You really do not understand what it is to be a walking corpse, do you? Of course, I would happily remedy that," I replied flexing my bone fingers in anticipation.

"Later, my good fellow," he said with a casual wave of his hand. "I need to find this egg. You know, you are interested in discovering new and unique aberrations. What do you think will hatch from such an egg? After all, the Easter Bunny is a boy rabbit, and the last I heard, rabbits don't lay eggs, especially boy rabbits. I acquired the egg by giving up my spring edition of Lapis Ladies Lingerie. He was so excited by the prospect, the egg just popped right out of him."

"Usually it is something else that is brown that pops out of animals."

"Ah, but this was real chocolate, believe me! I know chocolates!"

I threw down my pen. Gathering up my staff, I pulled myself to my feet. "I yield! I will help you look for this accursed egg, but you will have to leave me be for a whole month."

"Agreed!" he answered quicker than I was comfortable with.

2

We made our way to Nikodemus' room. My lair in the tower was meticulously neat and organized. Everything had a place. If I needed to find a spell or a component for an experiment, I could easily access it. Nikodemus' abode was a completely different story. How could I begin to describe this chaos? Granted, I was not alive, and I had no need for food, dirty clothes, or picture books for male entertainment, but even if I did, I doubted that I could make such a mess. The room looked like a dragon had gone on a rampage through it in search of a tasty knight. The Shadow Servants of the tower, who did the housekeeping, only threw up their hands and left the master to his own devices.

Despite the vast entropy that was before me, I was relieved to observe no signs of vermin, who delight in such environments. Everything seemed to be dead and inanimate around us. If it were dead, it could stay that way until I chose to control it. I wanted nothing to do with anything that was not animated by my own hand.

Although trying to look at and sort out all the chaos gave me a headache, the little wizard hopped into the mess and led me through the maze. At the end of the trail was a huge, brightly colored basket, large enough to carry away my companion . . . if only I were so lucky. Strands of green, shiny paper fell out of the basket, as if some creature had burrowed into the interior to make a nest. Clenching my jaw tightly, I cast the spell that told me how many lifeforms were in this basket, living and undead. My shoulders and back relaxed. Nothing was alive in it.

Feeling much more comfortable, I bent over and picked up a strand of the paper and ran it through my fingers. It looked like grass, but it was thinner and lighter than any plant material. It also had no moisture and was transparent. There was nothing organic about this substance. Looking around, I found a piece a bit thicker and greener than the rest. I picked it up. It was rolled and melted into a lump, as if it had been burned. Even the tang of a chemical reaction remained. Could some grand wizard have tried to hatch this egg by using explosive alchemy? What was this egg? No telling with Nikodemus' tendency to collect things (especially things that were not rightfully his).

I examined the basket next. Again, it was not of any kind of living matter. It was solid, but made of some soft, flexible material. Traces of a foreign magic still clung to it. I pulled myself up straight and looked down on Nikodemus.

"Is this some kind of dimensional coach of yours? If we climb into it, will it take us to that dreaded place of happy blue birds and rainbows?"

"Nah," he answered, ignoring my condescending tone. "The tower does not take too well to dimensional travel except its own."

"And what do you suppose happened to the egg?" I asked.

"I don't know. That's why I asked for your help." He moved with the speed that only those of fay blood can and grabbed my arms. Looking up at me with big, pleading brown eyes that reminded me firmly of a cow headed for the slaughter, he beseeched, "Please, Mal! You have to help me! The Easter Bunny is a big boy, and he will thump me if I lose his egg. It isn't easy for a boy to lay an egg that big!" He spread his arms out wide to indicate the egg almost as big as himself.

"And I am helping you for what reason? If you die, I can have your tower without your asinine rules."

"Ah, come on, Mal. Are my rules that hard to follow?"

"For a lich, yes. I should be the one making the rules. The bloody Abyss! I commanded a dragon! That is no mean feat!"

"But you find indulging my whims to your advantage. You enjoy our dimensional travels as much as I do. Believe me, I notice that enthusiasm when you get the chance to show off what you know or have discovered. As far as the killing goes, I know a little about your history, and I know that you have always needed a reason to kill. That's one of the reasons I allow you here in the first place."

"Hah! What do you know of me! I emptied graveyards and commanded the dead there to do my bidding. I devastated armies, then made the dead on the field serve me!"

"Hush! Accept it. Who is to say that the next guardian of the tower will be as understanding of your unique circumstances and state of being? You may find yourself locked out of the tower or worse. The next guardian may be more powerful and righteous than me and wish to destroy all undead. Hark, my vile friend! The ice rats of Hell are coming for you!"

He did have a point. If he died without choosing a successor, I would likely find my situation most dire. It was the duty of all bloody goody goodies to destroy that which is evil, and there was nothing more evil than the undead. He had defeated me in a duel, a challenge that I made for possession of the tower. He could have easily destroyed me then and there, but he allowed me to study here and become a stronger wizard. It made no sense to me. When I became a lich, I accepted that no one would willingly help me. Yet, here I was, a guest in a place that housed all the magical knowledge in this dimension and many others. I could spend the rest of eternity here and still not learn everything the place had to offer. In many ways, I owed him greatly, but I could never let him know this. If I did, I would never hear the end of it.

Throwing up my hand, I went back to the work at hand. I made a closer examination of the basket and its contents. If I could find anything organic, I could squeeze some bit of information out of it. I was adept at divination. Things that once possessed some kind of life were like an open book to me. Honestly, most stories I could do without knowing. They reminded me much of those things that Nikodemus called soap operas.

Several colorful pebbles formed a path from the basket. Picking up one of these pebbles, I rolled it around in my hand. It was soft and waxy, but it was not hot or sticky like the wax from a burnt candle. With some concentration, I was able to delve my mind into its contents. Pulling back briefly, I gave a half laugh. There were enough chemical compounds in this piece to delight an alchemist for a year! All the same, it did contain a minute amount of organic material. It was such a small bit that my divination spell was barely able to work at all. The impression I received was darkness, then movement, falling, light, many bright colors, then stillness. I threw the piece down and stomped it. This was pointless. The organic component did not have enough substance.

Nikodemus found the trail and happily picked up the pebbles. He did a less useful thing with them. He threw them each up in the air and caught them one at a time in his mouth. Chewing on them like a cow with a cud, he stopped at the end of the trail. "Dimensional doorway!' he exclaimed, as he spat out the wad of chewed pebbles.

"Teleportation does not work here," I complained.

Teleportation was a spell that instantly took a wizard from one place to another. The caster had to know not only where he was headed but where he was starting. It was like a mathematical equation. You had to know the value of A before you could get to B.

The tower was a complete unknown that existed outside of all numbers. It had no value and all values at the same time. There was a room full of doors that lead to all dimensions imaginable. This was why my companion was able to drag me to completely different worlds, and he could meet the most absurd creatures like the Easter Bunny.

"Someone has bypassed all magical rules here, or he actually knows where here is," he answered. He threw another pebble in his mouth, then held his hand out to me. "Jelly bean?"

Ignoring him, "Are you not concerned about how someone can know that? Neither one of us has mastered such a skill."

"Can't you divine what happened so we follow him?"

"I am a necromancer, not a dimension splitter. I work with dead things, not the worlds they came from."

"Don't you know other kinds of magic?"

"I do, but I have much to study and learn. That is why I am here."

"Oh, I forget. You are a baby lich."

"I am not! I have been a lich for over 500 years! I am young, but I am by no means new to this state."

"You will just have to call up my old master, Xenopus. He was the creator of the tower, you know. He's sure to have the answer."

"Why would I want to go and do that? If he is half as crazy as you, I do not think I could stand it!"

"Aren't you a wee bit curious about what happened here?"

My shoulders dropped, and I looked back to the place where the trail ended. "Yes." Throwing up my fist, "I would like to know who has this power. I could blast it out of him, then I will obtain it for my own."

"That-a-boy, my power-mad megalomaniac!"

3

Before Nikodemus could plead for me to take him with me, I shifted my spiritual being into Limbo. Dimensional travel and teleportation may have been forbidden in the tower, but I was in a unique situation. I was dead. I could detach my spirit from my body to travel to Limbo at will. This was the reason I could go without Nikodemus, a more powerful and experienced wizard following me. The last thing that I needed was for Nikodemus and his master to get together and chatter like a couple of obnoxious morning birds. Given Nikodemus and the types of magicks he practiced, I had to wonder what kind of wizard this Xenopus was.

Nikodemus' master's idea of fun often consisted of taking his apprentice to something called an amusement park. From my understanding, this place was like a year round festival with happy people, fast rides, fun games, good entertainment, and tasty food. Nikodemus liked everything about the place, and Xenopus was fond of hanging out around the garbage bins. Hmph! My master's, idea of fun involved how many of my bones he could break without killing me.

Just because I could travel easily to Limbo did not mean it was a pleasant journey. Limbo was a bloody cold place, not a simple cold one could ward off. No matter what spells I cast or how heavy or tight my clothes may be, the cold wrapped itself around my body like some hungry python.

The only thing I hated worse than the cold was the fact that I appeared here as my human self. Stories tell that the soul is the reflection of who we really were. As disgusting as my human form was, I should have been the most terrible and vilest of liches. My eyes, ears, and nose were too big for my face, and I had an over bite that would do any jackass proud. I looked more like the village idiot than I did a powerful wizard. My lich form, even when I was a rotting carcass, was more pleasing to the eye. At least I could bear my reflection in the mirror. Hmph! No matter. I could not command the respect I deserved in either form.

Brushing my wild hair out of my face, I concentrated on the task at hand. The sooner I found Xenopus, the sooner I could get out of this place. With the proper movements of my left hand, I found the strands of magic around me. I pulled at the proper ones to allow me to call forth his soul.

"Xenopus! I call upon you. Come forward and do my bidding!" The spell I cast caused the winds of Limbo to blow around me in a sudden gust. Clenching my jaw tight, I braced myself against the cold. It would not do for me to shiver before the spirit I wished to control.

A figure appeared in the distance and made its way to me in slow, intermediate hops. Cocking my head, I raised my eyebrows at this strange sight. A frog-like being took form as it hopped toward me. Large, bulbous eyes atop the green head blinked sleepily. His wide, toothless mouth spread from ear hole to ear hole in a vast grin.

Above his lips were two slits for his nose. His bare, webbed feet flapped beneath red and gold robes. One hand was hidden under a voluminous sleeve. The other hand ended in impressive claws that could rend any flesh from the bone. He held a coffee mug that read "The Lily Pad Lodge" in friendly green letters. This was accompanied by a picture of a frog with female features, dressed in a halter top and panties. She lay across a lily pad with a mug in hand and a promiscuous grin on her face. From my association with Nikodemus, I recognized the smell of coffee with heavy cream.

"Eh? What do you want?" the creature before me complained. Blinking, I stood back. Something was not right here. I did not feel the power of control over his spirit around my fingers. He was here, but he was independent. Something else was wrong, but it was on the edge of mind and unattainable.

"You are Xenopus?"

"Yes."

"I command you to return to the World of the Living with me."

"Blagh! What do you think you are? Some grand necromancer?"

"Yes."

The eyes atop his head moved up and down as he made an assessment of me. His throat puffed out like a great bullfrog. He held it a moment, then he let go a humongous laugh. The tan liquid from his mug splattered down his ornate robe. Exasperated, I stomped my foot. Several devastating spells came to my mind, and they would be so much more effective in Limbo.

"Now, now, my good fellow, you made me spill my coffee," he commented, as he cast a spell that cleaned his robes. "Not that it was all that good. The Shadow Servants are nice enough fellows and excellent housekeepers, but they can't make a decent cup of coffee. I guess I should have given more thought in their creation and gave them taste buds." He grumbled several more comments, then he looked at me again. "What? You're still here! What do you want?"

"Someone broke into the tower and stole something. It was once your tower, and you should know how such an impossible thing could happen. I need you to return with me and open the portal again, so I can catch this bloody thief and blast his soul to the deepest pits of the Abyss!"

"You have some anger issues, don't you, boy? Why should I help you?"

"I could force you! I am an accomplished necromancer. It is what my bloody magic is all about!"

His eyes looked me over again. His throat puffed out like a straining balloon. Finally, he let it go in a croaking laugh. He tried to control himself and catch his breath, but he lost it. He fell over backwards and kicked his bowed legs up in the air.

"Do not discount me. I am a powerful wizard!"

"Yes. I can see that," he answered, as he righted himself. "But, my dear boy, I am vastly older than you and more powerful than you can imagine. Besides, I'm not dead yet. Even if I were dead, you would find me a hard one to control."

That was the oddness I felt about him. Spirits did not need to breathe nor did they normally have color. Only the living had color. He was here both physically and spiritually. Another thing occurred to me and made my insides clench. Nikodemus was a good 200 years my senior, but he was fey blood. They aged differently than humans. This was Nikodemus' master. He had to be at least 100 years older than him, and given Xenopus' achievements, I would add another two centuries to that. He had to be at least twice my age! Did anything actually live that long!

Throwing down my arms, I quelled my anger. I knew all too well my weaknesses. After all, this was why I tolerated Nikodemus and his pranks. Age in such beings was a great asset. The same could be said of the undead. I needed only to bide my time and bury myself in studies.

"You win. I will negotiate. What do you want? How can I persuade you to resolve this problem?" As I spoke to him, I never allowed my eyes to stray from his. He stood there impassively, and I could sense his vast power. Shaking my head, I knew my position.

My shoulders slackened, as if my puppeteer eased up on my strings. I lowered my head to his greater power. "Please. If you do not help me, Nikodemus will never let me be. How can I become a master of all magics if I am not allowed to learn?"

Light, delicate feet touched my shoulder, and whiskers tickled my ear. My spine stiffened straight. My eyes opened so wide, I thought they would fall out, and my fingers splayed. Slowly and rigidly, I turned my head to look into the beady, black eyes of my greatest fear. With the scream of bloody terror that would have done any undead proud, I swatted the rodent off me. Stumbling backwards, I needed a spell of searing destruction. I pulled on my vast store of magical knowledge. Everything was jumbled, but I gathered together the words of a spell. With trembling lips and shaking hands, I worked the magic. A puff of smoke appeared in front of my adversary and dissipated harmlessly into the air.

The rat only stood up on its hind legs and cocked its head. To my mind, it seemed to grow to a monstrous size to tower over me. The slashing pain crept up my legs and into my lower regions, where I had been chewed to death in life. I backed away from this apparition. My feet caught in the hem of my cloak. With flaring arms, I fell backwards.

This fear of mine made no sense to me. I was beyond the effects of rat fangs and claws. I wanted to curse myself and break down and cry, but none of this would serve my cause. I was never a being of physical combat. Much of this had to do with my size, or lack of it to be precise. I had always used my knowledge of the spell craft. My intellect was my greatest weapon. I had no choice. I had to cast another spell. My mind raced in frantic chaos.

My twisted tongue could not produce the words, and my trembling left hand could not find the correct threads of magic. Still on the ground, I pushed myself away from the towering fiend. My eyes never left this reprehensible demon. If I still had a real digestive system, I would have vomited and lost control of my bowels. Ice formed down my back and in my throat. My mouth gaped voiceless like a dying fish. Unconsciousness was not an option for an undead like me, but I desperately wished that I could lose consciousness just to escape from this gnawing terror.

Thin, clawed fingers wrapped around my shoulders. At first, I thought it was maybe some tentacle horror of Limbo. To have my soul devoured would be a thousand times better than this. The hands were firm, but gentle. Soft robes brushed my cheeks. No piercing claws or teeth entered my spiritual flesh. If it were not for every nerve being on edge, I might have found comfort in the presence.

"Ricky, come to me," the voice behind me called.

The rodent perked its ears and ran towards me. I twisted my body in an effort to free myself, but I failed. My imagination supplied me with the feeling of moisture under me and the smell of urine.

As it bounded beyond me, the rat paid me no attention. My head jerked like the cogs on the wheels of a machine. The little vermin ran up Xenopus' arm to his shoulder. I ripped myself free of his grip and crawled away on my hands and knees. The wizard, ignoring me, produced a peanut from nowhere, and the rat eagerly took it.

Laughing, Xenopus looked back to me. "Yes, you are indeed a fierce undead wizard, aren't you?"

"Shut up!" I spat. With a trembling finger, I pointed at the rat. "And keep that thing away from me!"

He laughed. "Come on. Let's go see that wayward prodigy of mine," he remarked, as he held his hand out to me.

Blinking, I looked up at him. The rat had disappeared. All that was left was the wizard. Spitting, I pushed his hand away from me and returned to the World of the Living on my own.

4

Awakening in the World of the Living, I found myself back in Nikodemus' room and sitting in a well-used, overstuffed chair. I shook my head and ran my hands over my body. Pulling my robes out, I gave a check to the inside of my clothes. My shoulders relaxed. I found no booby traps or compromising things on my personage. My thick, black robes were still intact, instead of some frilly dress, and I had no unwanted scents about me like a harlot's perfume or the stink of a skunk. No rodents scurried around in my clothes. Nikodemus had a strange sense of humor, but he had suppressed his whimsical tendencies this time. He really must have wanted that egg back.

Xenopus leapt to his apprentice and lifted him off the floor in a tight hug. Bah! What in the bloody Abyss was all this! I always wanted to blast Emeirikol to the deepest depths of Hell! I would never allow him to embrace me. Who knew what poisons were on the blade that he would plunge into my back or what vermin would appear in my clothes. Was it not the purpose of the apprentice to kill the master as a rite of passage?

Shaking my head, I pushed myself out of the chair. These folk were far too different for my liking. I grabbed my staff and waited for these fools to be done with their ceremony. If I still had saliva, I would have spat upon them.

Once all was said and done, Xenopus looked at me. The gaze of his bulbous eyes moved up and down the length of my skeletal body. Throwing back my head, I stood up to my full height. I was not very tall, but my straight legs made me stand marginally taller than him, and my macabre appearance was impressive.

"What insanity allowed you to bring this thing into the tower?" he asked Nikodemus.

I wished I could have smiled. Maybe he was different than the rest of these idiots around here.

"Hey! I'm just following your teachings. You told me to give everyone a chance. You never know what you might learn from the experience. Mal, here, he's a great source of information. Trust me. He's not as bad as he would have you believe."

"Bah! What do you know?" I said.

Xenopus croaked a small laugh, but his round eyes did not leave me. "Kind of small for a lich, aren't you? The staff only amplifies that shortness."

"Shut up!"

The rat poked its head out of his robes. With a curse, I pulled back. My feet tangled in a pile of trash, and I fell backwards into a collection of books with pictures of women in various states of undress.

"Oh! You brought Ricky!" Nikodemus exclaimed, as he took the rodent in both hands. He touched his nose to the creature's nose. I shuddered at the disgusting sight. I think I would have preferred to have a ghoul suck the marrow out of my bones.

Remaining on the floor, I could not bring myself to stand again. It would bring me closer to the rat. Making more choice grumbles, I pulled myself further back until I hit the chair. Nikodemus did something more heinous. He allowed the rat to plunge into the garbage. Screaming like a frightened child, I jumped into the chair. Grabbing my staff with both hands, I took up a defensive pose.

"What kind of lich is afraid of rats?" Xenopus asked.

"Shut up!" I cried out, as I looked frantically around myself.

Nikodemus whispered something to him. Xenopus stroked his throat.

"I see," he replied seriously. "That explains much." Keeping a straight face, he looked down on Nikodemus in silence. It did not last. His green jaws puffed up and out again. Cracks of laughter broke free from both of them like a great gale of wind. They both fell backwards in their merriment.

"Oh, do get on with the job you came here to do!" I demanded.

"Yes. Yes. In due time, my impatient child," Xenopus answered between gasps of laughter.

The two wizards collected themselves. The grins that crossed their faces threatened to break again, but they contained it.

"You are your own wizard now, Nikodemus," Xenopus said. "I do you no more favors. So, pay up, boy."

Undaunted, Nikodemus stood up to his full four foot height.

"Help me find where this dimensional doorway goes and retrieve the egg, and I'll take you to this nice, little coffee shop I found. They've got some sexy, young waitresses and a big aquarium with water frogs. I think if we hurry, we will make it in time for May Fly Day." Turning to me, he smiled wider. "You can come along, too, Mal. There are several books for your perusal, and I do believe they have bone china for you to play with."

"I do not think your idea of appropriate literature and mine are quite the same," I grumbled. Actually, the thought of spending more time with these two goofs with the rat in the middle ranked up there with attending a Kel concert.

"Well, my boy, you have a deal. I haven't had a May Fly Feast in an age! I'm glad to see you aren't just hanging around with dead things."

The thought of placing a curse upon him and his rat familiar crossed my mind. I knew a nice place that was ruled by cats, where I could trap them for a while. With the dimensional travel capability that Xenopus had, he would escape quickly enough, but it would be fun for a while. Even the dead need to dream.

The chattering of the rat brought me out of my reverie. It bounded out of a pile of papers far from me. Thanks be to all Abysmal forces for that! It carried a small flower in its mouth. The flower was a simple thing. It had a golden center with long, narrow, white petals surrounding it. With a leap, the rodent jumped to Xenopus' shoulder. The wizard took the flower from the accursed beast and twirled it around in his hand.

"Yes. Excellent work, Ricky," he said. With a wave of his hand, he produced several kernels of corn, and he gave these to the rodent. "Ricky has found the answer to your intruder's magic."

"Yes! Yes! Tell us!" I encouraged. "The sooner you get this done, the sooner you and that rat can leave! The Lords of the Abyss know that there are enough rodents here!"

Xenopus croaked out another laugh. "You could use some humbling, my boy."

Nikodemus shrugged. "He's a lich. He's bound to be arrogant. He's not near as bad as others of his kind, trust me. So, tell me. What did you find out?"

Shaking the flower at us, Xenopus flashed that frog smile again. "The passage was made by the one power that cannot be defeated. Flower Power."

"Lords of the Abyss! Not HIM!!"

"Afraid so, my boney, distempered friend," Nikodemus replied happily. Turning to Xenopus, he asked, "Can you reopen the portal?"

"Of course, my boy. Of course! If it has to do with dimensional travel, I can do it."

"Problem solved. Now I can go back to my work while you fools go play with the King of Fools," I said.

"Oh, Mal. Don't you want to go with us? Kel so enjoys your company. You inspire him greatly."

"I enjoy his company as much as I do a pack of ravenous dogs drooling over my bones. I did my part. So, go and take your rat friend with you."

"It's been forever since Ricky has been here, and I'm certain there are many new things for him to explore, especially in your room," Xenopus told me.

Grumbling, I called him something in my native tongue, which had been dead for a couple of centuries. His smile stretched past the edges of his face.

"Maggots make good eating, especially fermented in moose dung," he told me.

Throwing up my hands, I gave up. "I will go with you. I guess I should see this through to the end."

Xenopus took the flower and shook it at the place where the jelly bean trail ended. With some concentration and a good bull frog croak, which sounded more like a belch than anything, he opened the portal. A swirling rainbow tore through the fabric of reality. I took a step backwards. If I moved fast enough, I could make it to the Hall of Doors and get somewhere far from here . . . away from this insanity and that rat . . . away from Kel. Granted, I was interested in all magicks, but some magicks were not worth knowing.

The rat bounded out of a pile of garbage. Losing all concentration, I froze in place. Xenopus' clawed hand grabbed my collar bone. With the flick of his surprisingly strong wrist, he threw me into the portal.

5

When I fell out on the other side of the portal, I stumbled. With some effort, I caught my balance and kept some dignity. Xenopus and Nikodemus slid out of the portal feet first into my back. I fell sprawled out with the two laughing wizards on tops of me.

"Whee! That was fun! Let's do it again!" exclaimed Nikodemus.

"Yes it was, wasn't it?" Xenopus answered, as he stroked his throat. "If I knew it would be this much fun helping you on this venture, I would have returned earlier."

"Get off me, you poofs!" I complained.

"Oh, pardon us, your vileness," Xenopus said, as he bounced away from me.

Nikodemus rolled off me then offered me a hand up. With a growl and a foul word, I shoved his hand away. I pulled myself up on my own.

We found ourselves in a smallish room lit by multiple sparkles of light. These danced around the small space in ever changing colors, as if to hypnotize the onlooker. Although the light distorted the vision of normal folk, I could see clearly. Splotches of paint decorated the walls as if there had been a great food fight here. Periodically the paint congealed into something recognizable. Several symbols that looked like a splayed turkey foot in a circle were drawn in random places, but most of the images looked like a five year old's attempt to draw rainbows, butterflies, and unicorns.

In one corner was a large, framed portrait of a dark skinned man, wearing that turkey foot symbol about his neck and on his headband. He wore colorful clothing and held a guitar that was strung upside down.

In the middle of the room, sitting on overstuffed pillows was that blue haired half elf known as Kel. The lights played over his pale face and pointed ears. He held out his delicate hands to his sides with the wide sleeves of his colorful shirt hanging peacefully. His hands formed an "O" with his forefingers and his thumbs.

Ragged hemp pants covered his legs which were crossed under him with his bare feet in his lap. A cigarette hung from his mouth and emitted a foul smelling smoke that outlined him and the chocolate egg under him.

Rolling up my sleeves, I had the perfect spell in mind that would summon some horrible monster from that egg. It could eat him, foul tobacco and all. After all, he did invade the place where I resided and stole something. That was enough reason to kill him, yes? Nikodemus smacked my hands down.

He reprimanded, "Behave yourself."

Kel's spacey blue eyes opened wide and so did his mouth. The cigarette fell out and into the pillows, where it smoldered. If luck was with us, the place could become his funeral pyre.

"Hey, Kel!" Nikodemus hailed him. "Can I have my egg back?"
Kel clucked like a chicken ready to lay an egg. Cocking my head, I knew he already had. Yes. I resided in a ridiculous world.

"Cluck! Cluck! Per Pluck!
I laid an egg!
How truly amazing, man!
'Cause I'm a dude!
Now I must hatch it!
And my little chick may come out and lay me!"

He had to sing! Could things get any worse? His voice had the quality of the creature from the deepest pits of the Abyss screaming out its death throes. The only thing that made this tolerable was the lack of any kind of musical instrument for him to torture.

He looked around at his audience. Nikodemus knocked my hands down again. What good did it do me to have all these spells at my command but not be able to kill anyone?

"Why can I not blast him? It is self-defense! I need to protect what little sanity I have left," I complained.

"Hush! It's not that bad," Nikodemus answered.

"Hey there, Nicky! Hey there, Grateful Dead dude!" Kel paused a moment, and his stoned eyes opened wide. "Hey! Jeremiah! I haven't seen you in like forever!"

"I'm not Jeremiah. He's my cousin," Xenopus answered, as he looked up from his examination of a half-eaten sandwich.

Before more useless conversation could carry on, the egg began to shake and rattle. Kel's mouth formed another "O" and his eyes opened wide. The egg bounced and bucked him off. Kel flew across the room and landed upside down in front of the picture of the musician. His legs spread out in a "V" above him.

The shell of the egg fell away to reveal its vast, horrible secret. What hopped out of the remains was truly horrendous to see. It gave me a gleam of the reason why these people did not fear me.

In this world, there were creatures called halflings. In some distant past, the gods decided to make a cute, cuddly creature that was a cross between childlike human and a rabbit. Halflings were the result. They stood almost three feet tall, have large, soulful eyes and long ears, but they had the laughing mouth and nose of a mischievous, happy child. Mostly what they were good for was eating everything in the house and burrowing. One of my previous associates claimed they made for good hors d'oeuvres. I guess halflings were marginally better than goblins, which were only good for target practice.

The halfling that emerged from the shell was a normal enough specimen of the species, except he wore an outfit similar to Kel's and he carried a bulging bag on his back. Dried weeds fell from this sack as he bounced over to the fallen bard.

"Little Weed! My groovy, main man!" Kel exclaimed as he righted himself in a smooth, fluid motion like blood flowing from a corpse. He slapped hands with this vermin of a creature. "Where have you been, man? Smokey's getting mighty anxious about his shipment."

"You know how it is, dude. The Man got whiff of the job, and he was hot on my bunny trail! So, the Easter Bunny gave me the perfect hiding place in exchange for some of that special lettuce."

"We'd best hurry! Smokey has threatened to send out his 10,000 vicious butterflies if you didn't deliver soon! They do make one mighty itchy when they get all inside your clothes and all! I got a bunch of them in my boxers once, and . . ." Kel explained.

"Then it'd be best not to keep him waiting!" Little Weed agreed. He pulled out a flower like the one Xenopus' rat had found in Nikodemus' room. He shook it in a corner, and another portal appeared. Kel and Little Weed jumped into it. The portal closed up behind them. Yeah, like anyone would really want to follow them.

"Well, I guess the Easter Bunny won't be getting his egg back," Nikodemus remarked, as he looked over the shattered remains of the chocolate.

"It was all part of the plan, my boy. The Easter Bunny would be proud of you," Xenopus said.

Shaking his head, he took a piece of the chocolate and put it in his mouth. "It was mighty good chocolate though. It's a shame to let it go to waste."

"I'm certain Kel and Little Weed will take care of it once they are done with their mission. That tobacco makes one mighty hungry. Come on. Take me to that coffee shop."

"Yes," Nikodemus replied, completely forgetting the drama. "Coming, Mal?"

"I think not. I have had enough foolishness to last for several lifetimes. I think I will walk home and visit the book store in town."

"Have it your way," Nikodemus answered. Xenopus opened a new portal and the two of them disappeared in it.

Shrugging, I knew it was time for me to make my departure. Since Kel was the resident bard at the Purple Unicorn, I knew his room in that dive. I was on good terms with the proprietor Jeriah, Perhaps I could convince Jeriah that he could put Kel's frog garden to good use. A frog leg eating contest seemed like a good idea. I would enjoy watching the riff-raff of this town eating their full and think of Xenopus.

Now I knew what the result of the chocolate egg laid by the Easter Bunny and hatched by a Kel was. I think I could have done without that information.

A KNIGHT FOR ELIZABETH

By *Mikey Chlanda*

Elizabeth and I were walking over to Molly Malone's to have the weekend brunch special. As we came up on 8th Street, we noticed an abandoned electric wheelchair sitting at the corner, like it was waiting for the bus. We looked at each other in puzzlement. How the hell do you lose your wheelchair?

Did the owner look on the bus, notice all the seats, and just said the hell with the wheelchair? Was it an alien abduction? Was it the healing power of forties consumed on a Sunday morning? Whatever the reason, there was one thing for sure – like John Callahan said, "Don't worry, boys, he won't get far on foot."

With a look of "I knew it!" Elizabeth laughed as I whipped out my phone and stepped in the street to take a picture of the lonely wheelchair.

I started crossing the street when I noticed a guy with a prosthetic leg making his way up the block towards me, waving his arms furiously, and grunting. I didn't think anything of it – hey, I'm from New York – and kept crossing the street.

Then I noticed Elizabeth was not with me. I turned around in the middle of the street and saw Elizabeth still standing on the corner, waving her hands at me urgently. "Mike, watch out for that guy. I think he's pissed you took pictures of his wheelchair."

Still standing on the center yellow lines on 8th Street, I was insulted.

"I'm a firefighter!" I said. Gesturing at the one-legged man, now maybe ten feet away, I went on. "You don't think I can take this guy? He's got one frigging leg and he gets around in a wheelchair."

"That is so, so wrong." She laughed, shaking her head, knowing it was impossible to argue with me. She walked over to join me.

When we got to the other corner, the guy was waiting for us. It turned out that he had some pamphlets to show us and some pencils to sell us. We laughed again and shook our heads no, continuing our journey to Molly Malone's.

So there are three takeaways from this story. First off, you do not have to buy pencils from a one-legged guy if you don't want to. Secondly, the Sunday brunch at Molly's is delish.

And lastly, I will always be Elizabeth's knight in shining armor.

D. B. COOPER

By *Mikey Chlanda*

Chapter I

When the stewardess brought me the drink I ordered, I took it with my right and handed her my note with the left. She slipped the note into her pocket without looking at it, most likely thinking it was the name and phone number of some bored businessman trying to hit on her. I had to quickly tap her on her arm before she walked down the aisle so I could make sure she read it. The stuff they don't teach you in Hijacker 101. Jeez.

"Ma'am, you're gonna want to read that note." I whispered to her. "I have a bomb."

Her face turned ashen as she retrieved the paper from her pocket. "I have a bomb in my briefcase." the note read. "I will use it if necessary. I want you to sit next to me. You are being hijacked." When she finished reading it, she turned around and hurried toward the cockpit.

Awaiting her return, I sipped on my bourbon and soda, took out another Raleigh and lit up.

When I saw her coming back down the aisle from the cockpit, I moved over to the window seat, putting the paper bag between my leg and the wall of the aircraft and placed the briefcase on my lap. I reached into the bag and took out the sunglasses, putting them on. Hopefully she was too nervous earlier to not notice my eye color.

As she gingerly sat down next to me, she said, "They want to know if you really have a bomb."

I nodded and opened the briefcase about half way, showing off the dummy bomb I had concocted with the play dynamite, a dry-cell battery, and some wire to connect it all.

I asked her to give me back my note, remembering that I had written it before I put the clear fingernail polish on my fingers to cover my prints. Whoops.

Then I told her, "I want you to write out some more notes for me, understand?"

She nodded and replied, "Yes." She reached into her pocket and took out a pencil and some paper.

"Write this down," I waited a minute for her to get ready. "I want $200,000 in cash by five p.m. today. Put it in a knapsack. I want two back parachutes and two front parachutes. When we land, I want a fuel truck ready to refuel. No funny stuff or I'll do the job."

She wrote down what I told her and showed it to me. I nodded approval and she got up and walked back towards the cockpit.

After a few minutes, the pilot came on the P.A. System to announce that they had some mechanical problems and the landing would be delayed. Good, I thought to myself. This way I didn't have to worry about any passengers acting like swaggering cowboys.

Looking down to the ground all lit up, I remarked, "This looks like Tacoma." One of the other stewardesses jumped back in surprise. I winced, not realizing I had said it aloud. A dumb mistake. I couldn't afford more of those.

Finally another stewardess came back with the news that they were working on assembling the money and the chutes at Sea-Tac airport.

She seemed a lot less nervous than the first stewardess.

"What's your name?" I asked her.

She replied, "Tina."

"Okay, Tina. I want you to go ahead and tell the pilot I want him to land now. Then come back and sit with me, in the aisle seat."

She nodded and scurried off to tell the pilot.

After landing, I told Tina I had a few more messages for her to relay to the pilot. Once I got the money and chutes on board, I would release the passengers and part of the crew, except for her and the pilots. I wanted the lights dimmed in the cabin and the shades pulled down on all the windows, in case the FBI had sharpshooters aiming to shoot me. And I wanted meals to be brought on for the remaining crew –they had to be starving by now. A half-hour puddle jump had turned into an almost three hour flight.

After what seemed like an eternity, I saw a baggage truck pull up to the front passenger door. I sent Tina up there to fetch the money and the chutes. It took her two trips to ferry it all back to where I was sitting. With the plane only one third full there were plenty of empty seats. She put the money bag in the seat next to me and the chutes in the seats in front of me.

I noticed the cash was all in twenties. Shit. I was expecting hundreds – and it was in a canvas mailbag, not a knapsack like I had requested. Obviously it was a lot heaver. I was going to have to figure out something because I couldn't carry that bag down with me.

Meanwhile, the fuel truck seemed to be taking forever. I sent Tina up front to find out what the delay was. She came back to tell me the fuel lines had frozen up.

"Bullshit!" I lost it. "You expect me to believe that? Jet fuel doesn't freeze in this weather – it's gotta be a lot colder. Now get the show on the road or I'll blow up this damn plane now!"

Tina shuddered and went back up to the cockpit to relay the message. Within minutes, she returned to announce the fueling had restarted.

I turned to Tina. "Tell the pilot we're heading to Mexico City."

She scurried up the aisle to deliver the newest message. When she came back, she leaned against the seat and asked, "Why are you hijacking this plane?"

I wanted to be a smart-ass and say, "For the money, darling." But instead, I said, "I don't have a grudge against the airline, or anyone else. I just have a grudge."

While we were on the ground in Seattle, I had wanted the pilot to take off with the stairs down.

"Okay," I said. "Go tell the pilot to fly below ten thousand, and keep the cabin depressurized."

"Anything else?" Tina asked.

"I want the landing gear down and tell him to set the flaps at fifteen degrees."

Tina played messenger at the beginning as I negotiated with the pilot. But when I demanded we take off with the aft stairs deployed, the pilot came down the aisle to talk to me in person.

"I can't take off with the aft stairs deployed. It's not safe," he said. "They can be opened once we were airborne."

I disagreed with him but I didn't want to push it too much. The more time we spent on the ground, the longer the FBI would have to figure out what I was up to and organize search parties. "Okay, we take off with the stairs up. What else?"

"With Mexico City as a final destination, we won't be able to get there without stopping to refuel, since having the flaps set and the wheels down will mess with the fuel economy."

"What's the maximum range with a full tank?" I asked.

"Flying like this, maximum would be no more than a thousand miles."

"Will that get us to Phoenix?"

"Reno is a better option."

"Okay." I didn't press the point, as I planned to be on the ground long before we got anywhere close to Reno. With a few hours to plan it, I was betting they would lay a nice trap for me wherever the refueling point would be.

The truck finally finished fueling and I released the passengers and crew as promised. Soon we were in the air again. As we gained altitude and headed back towards Portland, I looked at Tina and pointed at the aft stairs. "You're going to show me how to open them."

Tina nodded.

After she showed me how to lower the stairs, I surprised her by pulling two bundles of the ransom money from the bag.

I motioned to her. "Take it," I said, "it's yours." She just shook her head and bit her lower lip.

I sighed. "All right then. Go up front and stay with the others and close those curtains." The last thing she did before she closed the curtains between the first class section and coach was to take one last look at me. I never did know what to make of the look she threw me.

I put on one of the main backpack-type parachutes. I chose the older military-type chute packed in what we called an 'NB-6' container back in my Airborne days. The other chute must have been a newer civilian type. This was no time to messing around trying to learn a new chute rigging.

The pilot paged me on the intercom. "Anything else we can do for you?"

"Nope," I said, busy getting ready for my first jump in many moons.

I arched my back and cinched the straps tight. When I picked up one of the emergency chutes, I got a good laugh. The emergency chute was a training chute that didn't work. I decided to use it and take a chance – after all, no experienced skydiver would knowingly don a dummy chute, right? Let them try to suss that one out.

I tossed the sunglasses into my briefcase. Then I pulled the ripcord on one of the other chutes. Pulling out the parachute material, I used my Swiss army knife to slice a few long pieces of cord from it. It was tricky to use parachute cord for tying things together, but it was strong. After all the trouble I went through to get the money, it'd be a pisser to lose it while making good on my getaway. I tied another piece of cord around his waist, leaving several feet of slack.

I took off that stupid clip-on tie and threw it onto the seat. Then I tied the briefcase and the bag with the money together with several more pieces of cord. When I was happy with the way they were secured together, I took up the slack cord that was tied around my waist and tied it to the moneybag/briefcase combination. I double-checked everything – I didn't want to screw up anything now that I was in the home stretch.

Following Tina's directions, I got the aft stairs lowered. It only went down a few feet, held up by the air currents blowing around the plane. I tested the steps with one foot, and then I started down, gripping the handrails tight.

The wind was whipping through my suit as I made my way down. Jeez, I should have asked for a winter coat along with the ransom money. At the bottom of the steps, I gave the parachute straps one last tug and made sure the dummy emergency chute was secure on my chest. Like it was really going to help me, being a dummy chute, if my main chute failed to deploy. I did glance off to my right to make sure I could see I-5 and get my general bearings.

I didn't bother to stop at the edge to look – what the hell was I going to see in darkness over a large forest in the middle of nowhere?

Then I walked off the ramp into darkness, ripcord in hand, awaiting my next adventure.

Chapter II

Call me D.B. What the hell, that opening line worked for Melville. "Call me Ishmael." He sold a boatload of copies, if I can believe my high school English teacher.

It's not D.B., anyways. I signed the airline's passenger manifest "Dan Cooper," but my handwriting was so bad, the FBI took it as "D.B. Cooper." Whatever. Might explain why they can't find enough shit on Trump to impeach his ass.

And to be totally honest, my real name is not Dan Cooper or D.B. Cooper, either, for that matter, regardless of what the FBI claims. But I am not going to tell you my real name – that's not the point of this book.

This book is about how I walked out of my life, hijacked a plane, parachuted away with $200,000 of the government's money, and lived to tell about it.

For the first forty-something years of my life, I played the game by the goddamn rules society set up. I went to a good school, majored in business, and married my college sweetheart. I did a short stint in the army to repay them for my college education, and got a job managing a small chain of hardware stores in the Midwest.

Then in the 1970 Wal-Mart was getting started on their expansion plans to go national. Slowly they located stores in the towns we were in, or in the next town over. People starting shopping there, falling for the everyday low price bullshit, not realizing that all the shit was made in China by a guy making a buck fifty a day. They didn't realize by buying stuff there, they weren't supporting American workers actually getting paid a middle-class wage with benefits in American factories. Or stores, for that matter.

The pincers started closing in on my company. They decided they didn't really need a district manager when there was only store left in the district to be managed.

There I was, forty-four years old, laid off, no pension because the company drained it to pay their bills just before they went bankrupt. My wife left when the good corporate job dried up – I can't say I blame her. She did stay around long enough to see our kids through college – kudos to her for that.

So I decided to borrow on my Airborne experience from the Army, hijack a plane, and parachute away into a new life.

Here I am, fifty years later, wanting to tell the story. I'm eighty-four – about goddamn time I told someone the story. Hell, by the time this book comes out, I'll probably be dead. According to Warren Zevon, that's when you sleep. Taking his advice, I am busy living life. I'll sleep when I'm dead.

If you want to blame me for the increased security at airports, go right ahead. When I pulled my stunt, we didn't have any airport security whatsoever. You could go ahead and get on the airplane with anything you wanted, aerosol sprays, all the liquid mouthwash you wanted, whatever you wanted. Or you could bring a briefcase full of pseudo-explosives on board and hijack the plane, like I did.

That kind of backfired on me, by the way. With the tightened-up ID requirements, it makes it kind of tough for me to get on airplanes, rent a car or whatever. For some reason, the government is making it tough for us fugitives to fly anywhere. What's up with that?

So this is my story –how a middle-aged unemployed worker-bee that played by the rules stuck it to the *MAN*. One small win for the common man.

NOT SCRUFFY

By *Barbara Howard*

"Hooooooooowl! Hooooooooowl! Hooooooooowl!"

"Shut up, stupid dog." The old man shook his fist into the darkness. He stumbled blearily across the porch and into the house. The door slammed.

Scruffy whined softly. He was cold and thirsty. Circling three times, he dropped to the damp straw, sighed, and covered his nose with his tail. The heavy chain rattled as he scooted away from the frozen links. Wind blew through the door, ruffling his matted fur. Scruffy dreamed of a warm house, his mother's nudging nose, and his brothers and sisters.

The day broke gray. Tiny crystals of ice splintered the air. Scruffy checked the water bowl. Still empty. Snuffing through the icy mud, he found and wolfed down a frozen kibble. With a powerful thrust, he jumped to the top of the dog house. From that height, he could see across the field to the school. Children bundled in woolen coats with hats pulled low hurried down the sidewalk. He chuffed eagerly, hoping to see his favorite... the boy on the bike. There he was!

Each day, the boy rode across the field to join the girl and other children hurrying to school. It was weeks before the boy noticed him.

Scruffy liked the way the boy jumped from his bike each morning, and how his kind eyes held Scruffy's for a long time. He imagined the boy striding over to pet him, but he never did. He just looked. He looked even when the girl called, "Come on, Matt. You'll be late." Scruffy liked the way the boy always looked back when he jumped on his bike to join the girl.

Scruffy imagined what it would be like to belong to the boy. He would follow him everywhere, sit by his chair at dinner, and sleep with him at night, just like his mother had done with her boy.

The morning dragged on with nothing to do but huddle in the doorway of his doghouse. At times, a ray of sun slipped beyond the cloud cover warming him for a moment. When the blinking sun was high in the sky, the door to the house creaked open. The old man lurched across the porch, down the stairs, and into the yard, a cup of kibbles in one hand and a glass of water in the other. He scattered the food on the ground and poured the water in Scruffy's bowl.

Thirsty! Scruffy lunged at the water, jostling the man, spilling some on the ground.

"Stupid dog." The man kicked him. "I should just shoot you and be done with it." He slouched back to the house. The door slammed.

Scruffy lapped the water until his bowl was empty. He was still thirsty. Snuffing at the ground, he found every last kibble. He continued to search, hoping to find a few more, but there were none. His stomach growled, telling him he needed more food.

Jumping back to his roof, he waited until school let out. Most days, the boy called out as he rode by, "Hey dog! Good dog!"

Scruffy always wagged his tail, pricked his ears, and lolled his tongue, but the boy never stopped. He knew it was because the old man would chase the boy out of the yard.

The wind picked up as the temperature plummeted. Ice crystals turned to thick flakes of snow. Scruffy shivered. The chain hung heavy and the leather collar chafed his neck, rubbing the fur away.

Scruffy thought of happier times, when the woman was alive. She let him run in the yard and petted him. That was a long time ago.

The school bell rang. Children piled out the front door. Scruffy wriggled happily. Soon the boy would be biking by. He was so intent on watching for the boy, that the creak of the front door startled him. Staggering across the porch, the old man lumbered down the steps, and got in his car.

As the car pulled out of the driveway, Scruffy heard the boy call out, "Jenny, look! Old man Hubbard is leaving. Let's go see the dog."

Scruffy went wild with joy. He jumped from the roof of his doghouse and ran towards the boy. Reaching the end of his tether, he danced on hind legs. His tail wagged so hard that it whipped his body from side to side.

Approaching with caution, the boy extended a closed hand. Scruffy licked it, inhaling the sweet scent of sweat and dirt and boy. He whimpered. The boy's hand smelled just like his mom's boy. He licked harder.

"Oh Jenny... Look at him. He's so thin. He's shivering."

"Matt, the poor thing doesn't even have water. Ooh. The straw in his house is wet and dirty. Let's take him. I know your mom and dad would let you have him."

The boy unbuckled the collar, gasping at the oozing flesh below. He took off his coat and wrapped it around Scruffy.

Scruffy trembled and tried to pull away.

"Shh. It's okay. I'm going to take you home and give you some food and a bath."

Scruffy stopped struggling. He had to trust this boy.

Jenny wheeled the bike and Matt carried Scruffy. A long way. At last, they reached a small house with a fence around the back yard. Matt opened the door. Warmth flooded out.

Warm.

"What the hell is this?" A large man glared at them. Scruffy cowered and hid his head under the boy's arm. Warm pee trickled from between his back legs and trickled down the boy's pants.

"Dad, can I keep him? Look how skinny he is."

"Hell, no, we can't keep him. Take him back to wherever you found him."

The boy buried his face in the dog's shaggy coat and began to cry. Scruffy whimpered as he licked the tears away.

A woman entered the room.

"Mom. He's starving. Please, can I keep him?"

"Jim, I've seen this gray dog. He's the one that sits on his doghouse and watches the kids. Do you remember last summer? No shade except for inside the doghouse. You said he'd freeze come winter. You said something should be done. Well, here's your chance."

"Okay, okay, but give him a bath and comb that matted fur. He's scruffy."

After the bath, Scruffy drank three bowls of water and ate everything in the food dish. Padding happily behind the boy, he stopped when the small hand patted his soft, white fur.

"Look Dad, he's not scruffy at all."

AN ENTERPRISING NATURE

By *Brad Hudepohl*

When I was ten years old and lived on Glenna Drive, I found some wood scraps and built a small structure. I wrote my own skits and used my puppets to do a show for the younger kids in the neighborhood. The show was in the garage.

My show included the Three Stooges, a monkey and a chicken. I still have these puppets. Before the beginning of the show, I climbed into my small structure, opened the curtain, and would start the show. I also performed magic tricks. The children were always extremely excited about the performance.

I distributed flyers throughout the neighborhood that I had handwritten, having no copy machine. I charged a nickel for admission, and also sold lemonade for the same price.

When I was in my forties, I did a magic show with my son, Scott, for the kids in the neighborhood. This time I did not charge. Because we only had one trick. Scott would climb into a dog cage and I would lock the cage door. I had the kids check the lock. The top of the cage opened up, but only Scott and I knew this.

As I would put a curtain in front of the cage. I'd say, "Hocus pocus." Scott would climb out of the cage and sneak upstairs. "Hocus pocus," I'd repeat as the curtain went up. Scott had disappeared. The curtain went down again, and one more "Hocus pocus." When it went back up, Scott had reappeared.

OHIO STATE SWIMMING

By *Brad Hudepohl*

I started at Ohio State University in September, 1968. Three hours of physical education was a requirement. Ohio State offered a multitude of courses for the requirement. I chose to sign up for swimming. There were different levels of swimming: beginning, intermediate and advanced. All those who signed up for swimming had to take a test to determine which level of swimming to take. I ended up in the advanced class.

The class involved swimming several laps. It was exhausting; however, I enjoyed the feeling. Before each class, the diving class practiced. I arrived early and enjoyed watching the talented divers. Sometimes the diving coach conversed with me. Years later I saw this same diving coach on the TV as an Olympic diving coach for the gold medal winner Greg Louganis.

There were about twenty-five students in my class. I always finished eighth in races. I could swim catch up to those seven guys ahead of me. It was not until several years later that I found out that the OSU swim team practiced with the advanced class. I did get an "A" for the course.

HOME
A Personal Essay

By *Elle Mott*

Front doors to the women's shelter are ahead. Rain is in the air on this warm April day under Cincinnati skies. As I walk across the parking lot, two women look up at me from a courtyard off to the side. They're sitting at a picnic table, talking. One smiles at me. I smile back.

I enter the shelter and notice my steps across their black and white checkered floor. I look up. Women are congregating. Some are in the computer room, which has clear glass panes for its walls. Whereas, beige walls line the hallway. Some women are waiting for dinner, more than an hour away. The place sparkles with cleanliness. This is their home.

I check in with staff, and then join my friends in the kitchen. Savory spaghetti sauce is simmering on the stove top. Two friends have their hands in a big bowl of raw hamburger meat mixed with onions and seasonings. I wash my hands then dig in to help make meatballs. I smile. All is good for me on this day.

Come dinner time, women residents—sixty women in all—line up at our kitchen counter. We made so much spaghetti that there is enough for everyone to have seconds. Some women are quiet in approaching us. Having to depend on others for a meal can seem degrading. That is how it was for me. Some women speak up. "Bless you," "thank you for doing this," and "I used to make spaghetti for my kids all the time—this is so nice of you."

If only they knew, I'm the one thanking them. I used to be on the receiving end. More than one woman asks, "Are you a church group?"

I answer, "No, we are a group of friends who like to help out."

From my history of homelessness, churches seemed to be one of the toughest places to get help. Churches, it seemed to me, were always wanting something from us homeless folks in exchange for our place in their soup kitchen. Sometimes it was to show a wad of identification, as if we have a way to afford to keep our ID updated, not to mention safeguarded from rainstorms, or protected from theft. Lots of scary things happen on the streets to people who don't have a place to go home to; a place where they can lock their doors at night.

Another common expectation from churches was to sing for our dinner with praises to Jesus or reciting the Lord's Prayer before eating. It didn't seem to matter to churches that some folks identify as Jewish or of another religious or spiritual calling.

"Meatballs?" I ask. A young woman in front of me nods her head. Tom, who is on my right, passes me her plate, already laden with spaghetti noodles and sauce. I spoon meatballs onto her spaghetti and pass her plate to Chrissy at my left, who adds a slice of warm buttered bread.

This shelter does so much more than offer meals. It offers connection to community resources, medical care, housing assistance, and after-care services. This place empowers women. It is their refuge. It is a viable way to move out of homelessness and into stability. It is an opportunity to gain confidence in oneself and in the community as a whole.

My own self-worth had plummeted during our country's recession, a few years ago. Even with a college degree, I struggled for lack of secure employment. To not make rent payment is terrifying. If only, I could have come to this place when I had hit bottom in 2012. But, I was out west then, in Klamath Falls, Oregon. That place only helped men. Their city couldn't fund a second shelter; one for women.

That wasn't my first time needing shelter. The Red Cross helped me back in 2001 when displaced following an apartment building fire while living in Savannah, Georgia. Their help lasted ten days, not long enough for me to figure out my next move on my minimum wage income. Following a brief stay in my pup tent behind K-Mart, I then couch surfed awhile.

The early 1990s also saw me homeless. That time was a long stretch, with some nights under an overpass to wait out rainstorms. I felt lost in my life, lost in my purpose and felt invisible to city people. Looking for answers, I hitchhiked into Springfield, Missouri. There, a shelter helped me, and much like this women's shelter here in Cincinnati, it bridged the gap for me in my climb out of homelessness. That shelter gave me clothes, working supplies, and a sack lunch to take with me to my new factory job.

While women are thanking my friends and me for their spaghetti dinner, I too am feeling thankful. My time with them is a way for me to give in return for all the help I've received in my hard-luck times. I reply, "Thank you for having us."

Downtown Cincinnati sits on the state line to Kentucky. Across the Ohio River from Cincinnati is a sprawl of small northern Kentucky towns, which is where I call home today. My homeless days are behind me. Planning and action steps, accepting help, and a bit of my patience added in, brought me to this newfound confidence.

After our spaghetti dinner, I come home to my house. It's a small house with a fresh coat of yellow paint. Friends describe it as a doll house. It is an older A-frame cottage with an itty-bitty corner of a front yard. Flowers could bloom this year. I planted bulbs the summer before.

My credenza is the first thing I see when I unlock and open my front door. It is on the other side of the front room, at the opposite wall. I shut the door behind me and walk across my hardwood floors. I stop at my credenza to turn on a small wattage lamp that sits on it. I keep the evening light low. My pet finches—eight in all—are asleep for the night. Snuggled together, they sleep in nests they built from straw, yarn, and cotton. Their cage spans five feet, between my kitchen and bedroom entryways.

Framed black and white pictures hang on the side wall at one end of my credenza. When friends helped me paint this room, the paint swatch told us it was dove gray. It's a nice shade, blending well with my lamp shades, toss pillows and easy chairs. I chose an ombre of orange and yellow for my furnishings.

One black and white picture is a photograph of a bird on a tree limb. I paid only five dollars for that one. It was on clearance at an art store. Another picture, also achromatic, is of my father. I came to know and love him only after he died, but that's a story for another day.

Next to those pictures is the title to my house. It is also framed. It's on display, even if only to remind myself that today I have a home. No need to pinch myself to be sure. My home is clear of any mortgage. That took my sheer determination. I don't want to be homeless ever again over an apartment fire, or a recession, or any unforeseen mishap.

Sleep comes easy to me and I rest well following my evening with the women at the shelter. My bed is twin sized, but I don't mind one bit. It works fine for me and it is not a sleeping bag on a hillside of pinecones. Those days are gone.

Come morning time, I greet my pet finches. I'm okay that my house is small. It is perfectly sized for my birds and me. I open my drapes. Birds are feeding in the bird feeders right outside. My pet finches chatter back when the outside birds cackle. Across the street is a lake, which really is part of a golf course. Ducks in the lake let out their early morning squawks. The sun is out bright. Spring is finally here. And I am home.

'ALMOST HEAVEN' FOR SURE

By *L. N. Passmore*

The hills in West Virginia form a skewed checker board from one ridge top to the next, some folding, others crashing into one another. At the center of a half mile straight plateau on a narrow two-lane road, prone to heaves and disappearing shoulders, sits a hangnail house. Ruptured seams allow cats to come and go at will. Stubborn at heart, the place resists every attempt of the weather to beat it to the ground. About thirty yards from the house molders the ricketiest barn in all of West Virginia. Weathered and creosoted boards, rapidly turning into splinters, nailed to equally scarred anchor poles, make up its skeletal remains. Forget cats. A full-grown adult could easily squeeze through the breaches with nary a risk of a splinter.

Make your way behind the barn though weeds and elderberry bushes to a rising knoll. There you'll view a real treat—a mist-haunted valley that almost throws itself into the abyss. A rutted clay and gravel logging road runs higgledy-piggledy down to the creek. Along its banks spindly wild cherry trees with crackled bark sway and moan in the wind that wallops through the valley. Follow the creek to the sound of whooshing water to discover a waterfall. Looking closely, you'll see mink slides, but don't expect to spot the wily mink. They play hide-n-seek.

To the north and south of that high plateau between two villages, situated on the peaks of two intersecting ridges, the road careens up and down, curving like a contortionist. Although treacherous in winter storms, come summer, it turns into a shimmering glory road. All along the route redwing blackbirds bob on dented guardrails or wire fences and swing on tufted roadside weeds. Across from the east-facing front porch of the house and along the road, oaks and maples compete with fenced, terraced hay fields. At haying time, field mice scurry as the perfume of cut grass fills the air.

In a wide meadow beyond the fences, scarlet bee balm, Queen Anne's lace, and blue bachelor buttons host butterflies under a blazing sun. This patriotic spectacle runs down to a meandering stream, then up a grassed hill to the next ridge. Over that ridge, boasting one lone white stucco house, the sun rises. In winter it burnishes the crusted snow, but in summer its first gold-fuchsia beams wake the birds, set the crickets to nickering, and call home the cats. At night about eleven-ty-thousand fire flies zig their alluring lightning dance all summer. Brimming full moons hang so low their light floods the fields.

Heaven draws these hilltop homesteads up into the sky and fills the deep hollows with clouds that roll with the wind. At sunset they looks like forests of blooming apple trees.

"West—by God—Virginia!"

BLUE YULE

By *L. N. Passmore*

Jackson Burns dunked buttered toast into his glass of Southern Comfort and sucked the liquor-drenched butter before biting off a chunk. Chewing with the same meticulous attention he'd give to cleaning his rifle, he stared at the calendar with December 21 blacked out. The old moon's ghostly sliver of light spiked his festering gloom.

The radio pumped carols into his kitchen where he sat at a Formica-topped table. Waiting reverently for Dolly to finish singing "Hard Candy Christmas," he poured another hit of SoCo. With a tip of his glass to the blonde angel, he whispered, "I hear you, darling."

It was inevitable. Before he drained the glass, he heard "I'll have a blue Christmas without you . . ."

***

Volunteering for an extra shift at the mine, Jackie's dad left the house mid-afternoon, Saturday, December 21, 1957. He winked at Jackie. "Maybe a little extra to help out Santa."

By the time his mother cleared the supper table, Jackie finished his "Special Wish List," only possible when mine owners paid for additional work. The frigid weather guaranteed the mines were cracking. In full holiday mode WWVA's Christmas Countdown rocked the radio. Elvis' sexy baritone lamented, "decorations of red on a green Christmas tree, won't be the same dear, if you're not here with me."

Jackie cranked up the volume. "That's Mr. Blue Suede Shoes' new Christmas song, mom," he said. "He must love blue." They laughed out loud.

"I'm putting the album on my list." His eyes got wide. "Please mom."

With her husband working extra, his mother smiled. "We'll see, Jackie.

Just as Elvis got to "when those blue snowflakes start falling," a thunderous boom shook the house. Three successive tremors rattled the windows. They ran outside to the total dark of the new moon. Huddling together, they listened for the sirens. Without fail, their blare signaled the worst: mine disaster. Jackie's mom tried to call other wives but couldn't get through on Slippery Ridge's party line. They turned to the radio, hoping WWVA "50,000 Watt News" would give any report, any shred of hope the miners had escaped what must have been an explosion at Wind Grove. Nothing.

Frustrated in their need to hear what happened, they endured what seemed a lifetime of Christmas treacle, from the kid missing two front teeth to "Here Comes Santa Claus." Fan favorites Stoney and Wilma Lee Cooper, singing live on the Jamboree, crooned "Have Yourself A Merry Little Christmas." Jackie fought tears. Mrs. Burns clenched her bunched up apron and prayed.

At 10:03 p.m., WWVA's on the scene reporter, Chet Randolph interrupted the Jamboree broadcast. "Tonight at approximately 7:48 a gigantic methane gas explosion blasted Wind Grove Mine. Search and recovery crews have arrived at the scene of the catastrophe. Sheriff Jeff Morrell says it will take some time to determine if their mission is rescue or recovery. Stay tuned for more details."

"Scene of the catastrophe" reverberated in Jackie's head throughout the night.

***

The grizzled Vietnam vet poured himself another shot. He couldn't shake the sight or sound of Sheriff Morrell walking up to their front door on Christmas Eve. His black hat with the leather strap and big gold badge. His leather jacket with the official Sheriff patch.

His sad, sick voice. "I'm so sorry, Mrs. Burns. Your husband's body has just been recovered."

Fifty-seven years later, Burns still tasted the bitter tidings, the salt of his tears, and the peppermint candy he had crammed in his mouth.

RED HANDED

By *L. N. Passmore*

"Just what! Do you think! You . . . are . . . doing?" The woman in the flowered housedress loomed over the trembling child.

"Answer me!" The nails of her clenched fists dug into dishwater-reddened palms.

"Nothing, momma," murmured the five year old, who hung her head, keeping her own hands hidden behind her back. Suddenly her T-shirt and jean shorts seemed too tight.

"Nothing? Oh yes? Well, Miss Claudia Jane Tressle, just what . . . do you have . . . behind your back?"

The stale air of a melt-the-skillet hot August day grew thicker, weighing upon the mother and child. They both held their breaths. The mother's chest and neck burned, but Claudia's whole body turned cold. Her hands trembled.

"Nothing," Claudia said as she gripped the cloth tighter. Maybe it would magically disappear.

The mother yanked her daughter's bare arm, leaving behind a red welt. An empty clenched fist appeared. Claudia's other hand dug into her back. She looked up, eyes brimming, and shrank back from the grim stare of her mother's eyes.

The assault on Claudia's other arm produced the dreaded evidence of her crime. In her left hand appeared a mass of delicate, but crumpled, material. Pink. With ribbons. Some lace.

Her mother's hands shook, but her lips clamped into a tight white line. Tear filled eyes glared at the child.

Claudia looked up, pleading "I'm sorry. I'm sorry, momma! I just—"

"I don't care what you 'just.' How many times have I told you never to open that drawer?"

Her voice sounded like the grumble of their old Hoover

sweeper. The room began to smell like a dust-filled sweeper bag clogged with dog hairs.

Claudia shook her head, making tiny gold curls bounce. "I dunno." Then she held up four fingers and smiled, hopeful.

"Give me that!" her mother screeched. She snatched the pink fabric from Claudia then broke down, sobbing.

Horrified, Claudia felt sick in her tummy. "No. No," she whispered. "No throw up."

She held her breath and choked down that icky-bad taste every child hates. After taking a gulp of air, she said, "Momma? Momma, I just wanted some clothes for dolly. They're so pretty."

Claudia's mother wiped her eyes. "Well, they are not for dolly. They belong to. . . ."

"Who?" Claudia stood on tip toe and reached up to pat her mother's arm.

Mrs. Tressle held the infant-sized dress with the bows and double layer of lace to her face and breathed in the residue aroma, nearly faded.

She shrank down to the floor in a heap before her daughter and tucked her head over her knees, holding the baby clothes in her lap.

When she didn't answer, Claudia patted her head. "Who, momma?"

Mrs. Tressle raised her head. "Your sister."

"But momma, I don't have a sister."

"No. You don't."

NOTHING ABOUT THIS WAS FAIR

By *Gary Reed*

How Much Is Ten Billion Dollars?

That morning I arrived early – a rarity for me – at the campus of Xavier University, where I was commuter student. I went to the Musketeer Grill, got some coffee, picked up a copy of the Cincinnati Enquirer someone had left behind, and found a table. Before heading off to class, I got to spend a few minutes taking in some caffeine and the front-page news.

This was in the winter of 1968. The Vietnam war was at its most ferocious. On some university campuses around the country, student demonstrations against the war were commonplace. But not at Xavier and other conservative campuses. In fact, at Xavier and many campuses, Reserve Officer Training Corps or "ROTC" was mandatory for male freshmen and sophomore students. I was a sophomore.

Amid a controversial war, mandatory ROTC at 8:00 a.m. was not as popular among sleep-deprived undergraduate students as you might think.

On this morning, the instructor, an Army officer, began class by going off script. He said the Enquirer that morning had a story about a former Vietnamese Ambassador to the United States who was going around the country, speaking on college campuses. The Ambassador was telling students the reason so many Vietnamese peasants sided with the Viet Cong and North Vietnam was because landlords kept them poor and abused them. The United States, or so the Ambassador argued, should buy up all of the farmland in Vietnam and redistribute it so that the country's peasants – the great majority of all Vietnamese at the time. They would have a reason to resist Communism and favor the United States and its puppet government.

I could think of any number of reasons why that approach might not work, but the ROTC instructor didn't address the former Ambassador's argument head-on. Instead, he noted that according to the former diplomat, the cost of buying up all of the farmland in South Vietnam would be about $10 billion.

"Do you have any idea," the instructor asked, "how much money ten billion dollars is?"

The question was rhetorical, but I raised my hand anyway. I was sitting near the front, and the instructor called on me. The skeptical expression on his face suggested he was thinking, sarcastically, "Oh, this is going to be good."

I explained that when I left campus the day before to head home, I realized I was driving on fumes. I pulled my car into a little gas station near Xavier and gathered up all the change in my pocket, in the glove compartment, and in the crack between the seats. I bought eighty-six cents worth of gas, which got me home.

"So, no," I said, "I don't know what ten billion dollars in my bank account would feel like. But on the front page of the Enquirer this morning, the lead story is about an extensive effort by the Pentagon to determine how much the Vietnam War is costing the United States. According to the story, the Pentagon's best estimate is that, all in, the war is costing us about a billion dollars a day.

"If it helps," I said, "ten billion dollars would be enough to pay for our participation in the war for about a week-and-a-half."

The instructor smiled and gave a classy response. "Okay," he said, "you were prepared for me. I'll get you next time."

The News From The Home Front

I worked for and edited my high school newspaper and wanted to do the same at Xavier, but I also felt I needed a break and something less demanding as I adjusted to college life. So, during my freshman year at Xavier, I did news broadcasts on Friday nights on the campus radio station, WVXU. At the time, its signal reached the Xavier dorms and not much further.

Before my shift, I would stop by a nearby radio station and pick up an armful of teletyped wire service news reports the station didn't need. The long scrolls of paper repeated many of the same stories again and again. My job was to sort through them, select what I thought would make for an informative five-minute newscast, and then read the copy each half hour.

My most memorable experience was the evening following the assassination of Reverend Martin Luther King, Jr. Frustration with years of Jim Crow, redneck police with dogs and fire hoses, and all the other horrors of the Civil Rights movement exploded in inner-city riots across the country.

Classmates in the dorms called me, asking if I had more specific information than they were getting from television news reports about the disturbances. Worried by reports of rioting in their hometowns, they wanted to know how close the violence was to where their parents' homes were. I was sitting in a tiny room only a little larger than a phone booth, with no windows, no radio reception, and hours-old teletype-machine scrolls. I wanted to throw a brick through something.

Who Wants To Sign Up?

Later that year, the U.S. Army sent an officer to Xavier University to recruit ROTC sophomores to sign up for the junior and senior years of the program – the only years that counted for anything. For reasons I don't understand, the Army sent a soldier whose disillusionment with the Vietnam War was obvious.

"If you graduate from the ROTC program at Xavier," he told us, "the Army will send you to an artillery unit. As a second lieutenant in artillery, you will be a forward observer.

"As a forward observer," he said, "you will wear an eleven-pound helmet with an aluminum antenna that reflects sunlight and lets the enemy know where you are. The enemy shoots the guys with aluminum antennas first because they're officers and because they're the ones who can call in artillery fire.

"Your job will be to go to the front and beyond, looking for the enemy. If you find the enemy before they find and kill you, your job will be to call your location into your artillery unit, so they can shoot in your direction. If you're lucky, they'll hit the enemy and not you.

"There's a lot of demand in the Army for second lieutenant forward observers," he concluded, "because so many of them get killed. Who wants to sign up?"

Xavier Musketeer and ROTC Cadet Leader

Not everybody on campus resented the ROTC program or thought its purpose was to train men to fight an ill-conceived and unjust war in Southeast Asia.

Robert T. Rice, Jr., for example, was Xavier's top ROTC cadet. By all accounts, he was proud of the program and planned to pursue a military career.

No one shunned Rice for this. In fact, he seemed to embody what it meant to be a Xavier University undergrad. He was the

Musketeer mascot. At Xavier games, he wore a Musketeer outfit and led cheers. Everyone on campus knew who he was and liked him.

I, myself, had zero interest in the ROTC program to which Rice devoted himself. I also had no desire to be a career military officer, but knew the country needs people who do. I admired Rice's dedication and gung-ho attitude, but saw my life as having a different trajectory.

Rice was an upperclassman and graduated at the end of what was my sophomore year. I never got to know him.

The Xavier News

In my sophomore year, I began writing for the campus newspaper, The Xavier News, and continued in my junior year. At the end of my junior year, the university chose me to become the paper's next editor.

That was May 1970. The United States had just invaded Cambodia, and large numbers of students at Kent State University in Ohio demonstrated daily against President Nixon's expansion of the war. A friend, reporting for Xavier's campus radio station, invited me to go with him to Kent State to report on the demonstrations first hand. I was busy putting together a staff of student volunteers to run the newspaper. I was also busy with the usual end-of-semester rush to finish term papers, reading lists, and exam preparation. I declined.

A couple days later, on the exact day I became editor, Ohio National Guard troops opened fire on the Kent State demonstrators. They killed four students and wounded nine others, leaving one crippled for life. Some of the students shot had been demonstrating; others were watching from a distance or just walking across campus. In response, universities across the country erupted in demonstrations and other forms of protest. Many universities closed down.

The News from Pleiku

In the fall, I was a senior and busy with my classes and my responsibilities as the editor of the Xavier News, when a letter arrived from Robert Rice's grief-stricken father. Over the summer, in Pleiku in the Central Highlands of Vietnam, a mortar round had killed his son. Mr. Rice praised those who, like his son, served bravely in Vietnam and bitterly attacked those who protested the war. Like many in his generation, he saw those protests as unpatriotic and a slap in the face to those whose sons and loved ones served and died in that far off place.

A couple days later, a young woman stopped by the newsroom. She introduced herself as Rice's fiancé. She said she knew his father had submitted a bitter letter and wanted me to know there was more to the story.

During his time in Vietnam, she said, Rice had become convinced that the war was unjust and unwinnable. Even though he knew it would end his military career, Rice had requested a transfer out of Vietnam on moral grounds. She said he had agonized over the decision. Just days after she got his letter explaining all this, she learned of his death.

I encouraged her to explain that in a letter to the editor and published both Mr. Rice's letter and hers in the next edition of the paper. Together, the two letters expressed the strongly conflicting and often complex feelings so many had about the war.

Lt. Robert T. Rice, Jr. is one of the 58,318 names on the Vietnam War Memorial in Washington, D.C. A scholarship fund keeps his memory alive.

This May Be Dangerous to Your Health

My first editor at the Xavier News, Mike Henson, was brilliant but seemed to want the newspaper to be something of a literary journal. His motto was that the student newspaper "is not a bulletin board." Bill Barko followed him as editor. Barko wanted the Xavier News to be activist. His motto seemed to be, "Let's stir things up."

I learned from both but wanted the Xavier News to focus harder on being a newspaper – i.e., to focus on reporting what was news on campus. I also wanted the paper to be more widely read than it had been under my first editor, but more aggressive about finding campus news than under Barko. I suppose if I had a motto, it was, "Let's put out a paper people will read." Unfortunately, sometimes the desire to be interesting overrode the desire to be a newspaper.

One day, the ROTC department sent over a press release about a recruiting event for the ROTC program's third and fourth years. Some of the Xavier News staff might have preferred that I toss the press release in the waste can, but I felt the ROTC program was a legitimate, established part of campus life and deserved coverage, just like any other program on campus. I gave the story prominent attention, running it across the bottom of the front of that week's paper.

This wouldn't be worth recounting except, I didn't leave it at that. I wrote and had the paper run a little warning over the story. Like the cigarette package warning of the time, the banner read something like: "Caution: This program may be dangerous to your health." The stunt was stupid and sophomoric.

It was also not without consequences. It deeply embarrassed and frustrated the officer whose job it was to get the notice into the student paper. And it had unforeseen consequences for me.

Can I Enroll in Your ROTC program?

My draft number was twenty. That meant that as soon as I graduated from Xavier, my student deferment would end, and Uncle Sam would draft me, send me to Vietnam, and quite possibly, get me killed defending the corrupt South Vietnamese government. As attractive as that was, I had other plans. The University of Cincinnati Law School and the law school at The Catholic University of America in Washington, D.C., had both accepted me and offered me full scholarships. But to go to law school, I needed a new deferment. Attending law school was not a basis for a deferment.

I was more opposed to losing the opportunity to attend law school than I was to serving in the military. Re-enrolling in ROTC and taking part in the program's third and fourth years would provide a deferment. If I had to serve, my preference was to serve as an officer. With that in mind, I applied to the ROTC program at the University of Cincinnati.

My application arrived at interesting moment. Faced with student opposition to the program, the University of Cincinnati was reviewing whether it wanted to continue to have ROTC on campus.

The folks at the ROTC program submitted a routine inquiry about me to the Xavier ROTC program. They evidently got an earful. A stern, older officer let me know informally, not in writing, that I wasn't welcome. He told me the program would not turn me down – I think they feared I would raise a stink, and my rejection would become an issue in campus politics. Instead, he said, they would sit on my application and just never approve it.

If the University of Cincinnati had been my only option, I would have lost my scholarship, the chance to go to law school, and the opportunity to pursue a legal career. Instead, I would have headed off to boot camp.

The Air Force ROTC program at Catholic University not available to me, so I applied to the ROTC program at Howard University, the traditionally black university not far from Catholic University in D.C. The Howard University program seemed happy to have me. I joked about being the "token white," but I believe the program was just happy to make its numbers. For my part, I was happy to say that I had attended Howard University, even if only for ROTC, and to have my deferment.

Physical at the Pentagon

Besides classroom work, during the fall, the Howard University ROTC program required attendance at outdoor drills on weekends. I have had life-long problems with my sinuses and allergies, problems that are often at their worst in the fall and spring. On top of that, some of the drills occurred in bad weather. Predictably, I got sinus infections and missed a few classes.

Each time this happened, I made certain to get a note from the doctor at the student clinic at Catholic University attesting that I had a bout of sinusitis that required treatment. At first, the ROTC instructors at Howard were "cool" – assuring me everyone misses a class every now and again, and that I was doing well in class and had no reason for concern. I made it my practice to insist that they keep my doctor's note in my file anyway, just so no one would think I was a slacker.

Then, somewhere in the Howard University ROTC program, a light bulb went on: This guy is a law student. He's setting us for a disability claim.

I wasn't. I didn't even know that was possible. I *was* angling for another shot at the Army physical. But if they wanted to believe I was trying to lay the basis for a disability claim, well, that was fine with me. We want our military officers to have situational awareness and to seize the initiative.

My ROTC instructor told me he needed me to get an Army physical, to make sure I qualified for the program. They were sending some other people and he wanted me to go. He gave me the date and time.

With what I what I hoped was a straight face, I demurred. "I can't go then," I said. "I'll miss drill."

"It won't count as an absence," the instructor told me with some exasperation in his voice. "We *need* you to go."

The physical was in about a week-and-a-half, on a Sunday morning, at the Pentagon. If you were a college student in the late

'60s or early '70s who thought defending a corrupt, drug-dealing, dictatorial junta in South Vietnam was not wise public policy, the Pentagon was the very heart of darkness.

I went to the law library and looked up the regulations governing physical fitness for military service. First, I checked to see if the physical fitness requirements for admission to the ROTC program and Officer's Candidate School were the same as for the draft. They were. If you weren't physically fit enough to be an officer, you weren't fit enough for the draft.

Secondly, I found the regulations governing sinusitis, a condition just about everyone in Greater Cincinnati and Northern Kentucky has. I copied the regulations and sent them to my fiancé, along with signed medical records releases and detailed instructions concerning what I needed.

My fiancé, who was an x-ray technician, got copies of the records of my various surgeries and other treatments at St. Elizabeth Hospital in Covington. It helped that she had worked there. She also contacted my family physicians and got letters describing me as having chronic sinusitis. She sent the records Federal Express to arrive on Saturday.

My physical at the Pentagon was on Sunday morning.

The FedEx package did not arrive.

Saturday evening, I went to National (now Reagan) Airport and explained the situation. A guy who was not happy with what I was trying to do directed me to a jeep and drove me across the airport. As we zoomed across the airport, the passenger jets taxing around us seemed huge and to be coming at us from all directions. He took me into a warehouse, dug into a large bin of FedEx packages, and found the one addressed to me. Back across the airport we zoomed, with him explaining all the way why he didn't like helping me evade my military obligation.

The next morning at the Pentagon, things went as usual with the physical, except that the men administering the physical were doctors and corpsmen who took their jobs seriously – as opposed to

Cincinnati, where jaded clerks administered the physical and passed anyone who wasn't a complete train wreck.

At the end of the process, someone directed me into a room where a young physician looked over my results. He said I passed and asked if I had any questions.

"Yes," I said. "Could you put these medical records in my file?"

"What are they?" he asked.

"They show I have chronic sinusitis."

He glanced through the records and looked at me with a great deal of skepticism. "To fail because of sinusitis," he said, "you have to be really sick and not treatable by antibiotics."

"Actually," I countered, drawing on my first-year law-student skills, "there are two regulations dealing with sinusitis. One is for acute sinusitis. That's what you described. The other is for chronic sinusitis."

Another skeptical look.

"Those medical records show doctors treated me for sinusitis as a baby. And then, when I was a little older, they x-rayed my sinuses, thinking that might shrink my sinuses. Or something. When I was a kid, and again in the eighth grade, they injected some kind of oil in my sinuses. My family physicians treated me throughout high school and college. At Catholic University, I'm a regular at the health clinic."

I took a deep breath and continued. "Those records show that doctors have been treating me for sinusitis almost since birth, right up to last week."

I looked directly at the doctor. "Under the regulation," I said, "if you've had sinusitis your whole life, I think that qualifies as 'chronic.'"

"You're not getting out of the draft," he said and abruptly left the room.

I assumed he went to find M.P.s to arrest me, or to put me on a bus headed to boot camp, or something. He was gone about twenty minutes.

When he returned, he had a thick manual with the relevant regulations. He paged through it until he found the regulation for chronic sinusitis. He read the regulation, read the letters from my physicians, and looked at the regulation again. The letters, it turned out, were suspiciously word-for-word the same as the regulation. He looked at me and shook his head.

"You know if I say you're not qualified for Officer Candidate School," he said, "they'll just draft you?"

I forced a smile. "If that's true, then say I'm qualified. But I checked, and the requirements for Officers Candidate School and the draft are the same."

He looked aggravated. He spun around and stormed out of the room again.

After another twenty minutes, he returned. He said I was right, but he wasn't willing to say I didn't qualify. He was, however, willing to send me to a specialist.

The young doctor had one final comment. "Don't mind me," he grumbled. "I'm just pissed they drafted me."

I Can Get You In

I saw the Ear, Nose and Throat (ENT) specialist a couple weeks later at a nearby military base. He was a tall, quiet man who did the best ENT exam I've ever had. "I can get you in," he said. "I've put in your record that you're qualified."

I looked at him and said, "I don't think you understand. That's not why I'm here."

He looked at me, surprised.

I handed him a copy of the "chronic sinusitis" regulation and said, "Doctors have been treating me for sinusitis almost since birth, right up to the present. Under the regulation, your job is to decide if sinus problems extending over the whole of one's life qualifies as 'chronic.'"

After a discussion, he revised the sentence in which he had said I was qualified by inserting the word "not." He then turned the page over and covered the entire back with illegible physician scrawl. I assume he summarized my medical records, but whatever he wrote, it got me out of the draft.

And ended my ROTC experience.

In some ways, in presenting my case to the Army physicians who reviewed my eligibility for military service in 1972, I argued my first legal case, with myself as a client and stakes that, for me, couldn't have been higher.

Nothing About This Was Fair

One of the objections to the Vietnam War-era draft was that if you were white and from a well-off family, you could avoid the draft, but if you were black or brown or from a less-advantaged family, the draft took you (or you volunteered). My family was hanging onto to middle-class status by its fingertips, but I enjoyed many advantages that others, whose families were like mine or worse off, did not.

Most importantly, I was in law school. I could find and understand the relevant military fitness regulations and construct an argument for a deferment. My fiancé had trained at the hospital where I had my procedures, and she was working for the family physicians who had treated me for many years. She had the connections to get my records and the letters I needed quickly.

Even before that, I had had the good fortune to win a scholarship that paid my way through Xavier, deferring my draft obligation four years, and giving me the maturity to make my case to the Army physicians. And at Xavier, I also had the good fortune to take the initial two years of ROTC training, qualifying me for the program at Howard University. My ROTC classroom experience convinced me I could handle myself in a difficult discussion with a military officer.

Lt. Robert Rice served honorably and bravely, and died in far-off Vietnam in a war he came to believe was unwinnable and unjust. I too believed the war was unwinnable and unjust. I talked my way out of the draft, got my law degree, and have the good fortune to look back on all this fifty years later.

Nothing about any of this was fair.

BETHANY HEINEY

By *Alvena Stanfield*

Bethany held her security card high so the android managing the Dunbar Building entrance could scan her bar code.

"Welcome. Miss. Dunbar." The android said and, looking straight ahead, swiveled its head to verify she entered safely before it slammed the doors shut, locking them.

"Can I help you, Ma'am?" the guard behind a mahogany desk asked.

"Help me?" She pointed her index finger at her chest. "You don't know who I am?"

The guard's face flushed a blotched crimson.

"Sorry, Ma'am, no. Who are you?"

Bethany narrowed her eyes, waved her arm in a broad sweep toward the brass, marble, and glass foyer.

"Bethany Dunbar. That's who I am. Recognize the name?" She leaned closer. "Dunbar Building. Franklin Baldwin Dunbar. He's my father."

The guard took a deep breath and stared at her.

Shaking her head to bounce her curls, Bethany leaned close to him and pointed to her photo on her driver's license.

"Sorry ma'am, uh, sorry Miss Dunbar, I usually work nights. I'm filling in for the regular guard. His wife is having a..."

"Yeah, yeah, any excuse will CYA, won't it?" she said as she slammed her driver's license on his desk. "See my name? See my photo? Make a copy."

"Please Miss Dunbar, this won't happen again. I'll know you . . ." He leaned toward her intending to return her license. "Come back. Here's your driver's license, Miss Dunbar."

Ignoring his extended arm, Bethany checked her grandmother's antique watch and hurried away. Crossing the foyer to the elevators she glanced back at him. He was still holding her license above his head.

She tilted her chin and lifted her middle finger.

"Miss Dunbar, please stop on your way out to pick up your license," he called to her as the elevator door closed. Inside she leaned close to a mask containing eye scanners.

"Penthouse," she said and gripped the handrail as the elevator sped up the fifty-five floors to her father's executive suite. A loud whoosh of air accompanied the elevator door's opening, proof the compression triggered by the elevator's speed had been released.

The long hallway leading to her father's executive suite was lined with huge interactive video screens. Barely glancing at the assortment of industrial robotic equipment and metal robots a new video screen juxtaposed at the end of the hall caught her attention. With her hand on the identification screen at the entrance to her father's office suite, she glanced then stared at the hallway's massive interactive whiteboard.

The first image showed flesh-colors available, followed by color bleeds illustrating a wide spectrum from "Scandinavian Blanc" through "Nigerian Ebony." The second image featured two life-sized naked androids turned away from her. So lifelike their rounded butts and changing skin tones matched any seen at a nude beach.

Bethany touched the screen near the male android's thick and well-defined muscular back shoulders. Stretching upward, the android swung its elbows outward and flexed its back and upper arm muscles. It then bent on one knee, lifted its fist to its hairline and held the body-builder pose. Upright it slowly rotated 180 degrees.

Bethany gasped at its anatomical accuracy, including pubic hair. As the two robots rotated back to their original positions, a digital message crossed the screen: If you have to ask what they cost, you can't afford them.

"Only my sorry-ass brother would tack on a sarcastic message like that," she said to herself. A snicker from the receptionist alerted her she'd spoken louder than intended.

"I thought the same thing," Alissa said, pulling Bethany closer by motioning with her index finger. Crossing the foyer Bethany smiled, and tilted her head, hoping to hear office grapevine news. The view of Alissa's low cut blouse and bulging breasts pressed against the desktop told Bethany why her brother ignored HRs' recommendations and insisted on choosing executive staff personally.

"Your brother told me to check your purse, um, for flasks," Alissa whispered.

Bethany glanced at the ceiling and withdrew two. "Hide these, okay?" She blew her breath into her palm and sniffed.

"Sure, Miss Dunbar. But if he finds them I won't be the one under the bus, okay?" Alissa said as she unlocked her desk drawer.

"He can't smell vodka martinis," Bethany said as Alissa locked it and handed Bethany the key. Sliding a ten across Alissa's desk, Bethany winked at her.

"Both Mr. Dunbars are expecting you, Miss Dunbar," Alissa said.

***

Bethany gave both men hugs. "Thanks for meeting with me," she said, reaching into her purse. "FB, your receptionist tells me you're into checking women's purse linings now," she said and waved a Tampax.

Her father, Franklin, frowned. FB's face reddened.

"I have no intention of letting you waste my and Dad's time by showing up slurring and staggering," he said.

"That's quite enough, FB," Franklin said.

FB lowered his chin. "Step out of denial, Dad. She's done it over and over. Let me get a breathalyzer."

Bethany shook her head and sank into the leather chair in front of her father's desk.

"I didn't do anything, Daddy," she said and stuck out her lower lip, pouting like a four-year old.

"Just tell us what you want, this time," FB said and banged his ring several times on the desk.

Bethany twisted slightly in the chair and raised one eyebrow. "Well I love your new video wall." She took a deep breath, smiled at each man. "And, um, well, my ten-year reunion is next month and . . ."

FB grinned while glaring at her and tapped his temple. "Right. Let's see, that makes you twenty-nine, almost thirty," FB said.

Bethany lifted her middle finger and jerked her hand toward him. "Twenty-eight. So sorry third grade math is still a challenge for you, brother dear."

FB closed his hands into fists.

Bethany smiled at her father. "No, Daddy, my friends have real robots, but not as stunning as those." She pointed her thumb toward the office suite's hallway.

"So do you." Franklin looked toward FB, who nodded.

"That plastic-covered tin can? Sure, it loads the dishwasher, makes the bed and opens doors but it squeaks, jerks and makes clicking sounds." She pointed toward the hallway. "I want one of those drop dead, gorgeous male androids. And, uh, do all of his parts work?"

"That's disgusting," FB frowned. "But of course you would be willing to…"

"Just asking, that's all," she said, lifted her eyebrows, fake-flirting, smiled and blinked several times at him.

Franklin rocked forward. He winced and pressed his palm against his chest.

FB slid his chair closer to his father's and frowned at his sister.

"Dad, maybe we should take a break," he said, placing his hand on his father's arm.

Franklin shook his head. "No, I need to do this."

Bethany stared at her father. "Daddy, you're so pale. Why don't I leave and maybe we can talk about this later," she said.

"No, my dear, stay, and you can use your corporate card to pay for your…" Franklin hesitated, closed his eyes, swallowed hard, and slipped a nitroglycerin tablet under his tongue.

Narrowing his eyes, FB leaned toward her. "We have a new prototype we're developing. It will be perfect for you. I'll have it delivered to Kenny's apartment."

"To our apartment, FB. I can live with anybody I want, including Kenny." She looked away from FB, moved alongside Franklin and hugged him, ignoring her father's distress.

"Thanks Daddy. You wouldn't want your little girl to look like a pauper, would you?"

"I love you Bethany," Franklin smiled as she kissed his cheek.

FB scooted his chair back from the table, stood up and paced. He returned and sat alongside his father. "Dad, you can't be serious. The new humanoid robots are so costly to manufacture. Her corporate card is already 60% full."

"No, let her have what she wants. Raise her line of credit."

The elated look on Bethany's face alerted FB she could manipulate their father into concessions beyond any he would receive.

Bethany strutted toward the door and blew her father a kiss. Somber, Franklin opened a leather portfolio revealing stacks of notarized legal documents. FB coughed as he read "Dunbar Irrevocable Trust."

"FB, this business matter affects you." Franklin hesitated, took several breaths and tapped the table.

"I'm putting my personal estate into a trust to be shared equally between you and Bethany."

FB's eyes bulged. "Equal with her? Why half? She's already cost you more than half. I . . . I have cost you not one cent. I've worked non-stop to build this company while she…."

Franklin nodded. "Yes, and I agree you've been indispensable in building this corporation into a Fortune 500 company."

FB covered his eyes with his hands. "How can you do this to

me? She's done nothing but cost you money. She's added nothing to . . . I've . . ."

Franklin's face paled. "Unfortunately that is true. But don't forget I've paid you well for the many hours you've invested in this company."

FB began pacing, perspiration covered his forehead. "Why can't you just give her a stipend, a weekly allowance. You know she'll just blow her inheritance on booze or worse. When she's broke, then she'll turn to me to support her."

Franklin slowly shook his head. "You'll hate my other decision even more, FB." He picked up a thick legal document. "I am relinquishing my stocks and each of you will own fifty percent of this corporation." He slid the leather portfolio toward FB. "Here's the rest of my will."

FB scanned page after page. When finished he slung it away from him. He clenched his fists and leaned close to his father. Frowning, teeth clenched, he pounded the table.

"A million to Bethany's rehab facility? Get real, Dad. She's not rehabbed. She's a drunk and using. FB rose from the chair, moved toward the door. Arms crossed, he turned. "Maybe I'll take that offer Microcon made me. Their offer is still on my desk. At Microcon I wouldn't have to put up with a dead-beat partner."

"FB, I'm just trying to . . ." Franklin clutched his chest and slumped forward, his forehead resting on the conference table.

***

EMTs lifted Franklin onto a stretcher.

"He has a bad heart. He's next in line for a transplant but he's AB negative," FB said.

An EMT nodded and rushed Franklin toward the elevator. Chatting with Alissa, a shocked Bethany chased after the EMTs.
FB hurried toward the elevator as he dialed Franklin's cardiologist and watched the elevator doors close. Leaving the second elevator,

Bethany and FB ran behind the stretcher across the elegant foyer toward the front doors.

"Miss Dunbar, Miss Dunbar, I have your driver's license," the guard shouted, waving it.

Bethany ignored him and joined the EMTs sliding Franklin into the back of the ambulance. FB snatched the driver's license from him, and slid it into his jacket pocket.

When he reached the ambulance the rear doors were closed. Though the driver protested, he hopped into the passenger seat. FB demanded Franklin's doctors come to the hospital immediately.

***

After the EMTs began an IV, Bethany sat sobbing alongside her father among the tubes and wires hooked to him.

"Ma'am, please stop that. He needs rest. We'll take care of him," an EMT said as he gripped her shoulder, attempting to get more distance between her and the stretcher.

"You're blocking my way, Ma'am. Please move."

Bethany took a deep breath, pressed her lips tight. Sobs stifled, her shoulders shook as she continued crying and moved to the empty stretcher alongside her father's.

***

Pointing to a closed door, the Emergency Room clerk directed FB and Bethany to a small conference room.

"They will talk with you in a little while. Wait in there."

After five minutes of ignoring one another, an angry, red-faced FB began pacing.

"I can't believe he's giving you an equal share in a business I built."

Bethany shrugged and studied the ceiling.

"And he's sending a million bucks to that rehab center you went to. Worse, you get half of his billion dollar estate which we both know you'll drink away." He punched the air. "Worst of all, half the business, half of a business I've worked like a dog to build."

His face nearly touching hers, his scowl and the red veins in the whites of his eyes startled Bethany. Ignoring his distress, she shrugged, smiled, and returned to her magazine. She slowly turned its pages.

"You've failed at everything and lived like a queen on money I earned." FB waved his arms in the air. "Daddy this, Daddy that. Give me. Give me. Give me."

Bethany looked at him without lifting her chin. "And your point is?" She turned a page.

FB clenched his fists and took a deep breath. "You've done nothing, nothing but cause pain and expense. How can he decide to reward you?"

Bethany looked up from the magazine. "Huh? What surprised you about me getting my share? I'm his only daughter."

"Your share? I ... I've worked non-stop for him. Studied engineering. That's what he wanted. Not what I wanted."

"Well, it's not too late," Bethany said.

FB rushed to her and shook her shoulders. "It's too late for me. Who do you think will have to run the company now?" He beat his chest with his hand. "Me. Me, alone. There's no chance you'll ever be an asset."

Bethany shifted in her chair and slowly crossed her legs. "I've already been an asset. Daddy loves me just the way I am."

FB sat down, bent forward, and covered his face with his hands. "Eighteen years working for him. I was a kid with no childhood. No vacations. No holidays. I'm the one who went into third world rat holes to set up our satellite factories, not him not you. Just work, work, work." He leaned close to her. "I shouldn't have to watch you piss away half of what I produced."

She punched his arm. "So, maybe we can sell the company, split the money."

FB's bulging eyes alerted her she'd said the wrong thing.

"Split? Split? You've sat on your ass, mostly in bars, while I," he beat his chest with his palm, "I worked ten, twelve hours a day, missed out on holidays, cut our honeymoon short. Dad needed me to negotiate for him."

Bethany tilted her head, appeared confused. "I'd have worked for him if he'd asked me."

FB crossed his arms over his chest. "He tried to work you into the company. He started you just like me, in the mailroom. You drank your lunches, argued with experienced workers. You did even worse when he tried you in customer service."

Bethany shrugged. "It just wasn't for me. All that technical stuff and people whining if an order was late or wrong. They acted like each day was doomsday." Bethany looked at the ceiling and rocked her head side to side.

FB pounded his fist into his hand as he yelled: "You lost us customers. Delivery. Courtesy. Results. You violated every one."

Bethany returned to her magazine.

"That's what Neodynamics promises to deliver." FB grabbed her magazine and slung it across the room. "How do you think the company, any company, stays in business?"

Bethany shrugged. "How should I know? You and Daddy never let me in on any kind of planning or . . ."

"You should know. I shouldn't have to explain that to you. You caused a scene if anything annoyed you. Our customers lose money every time Neodynamics fails delivery or quality. It's so obvious," FB threw himself into a chair.

"Well it was never obvious to me," Bethany said, then leaned toward him. "Shouldn't you be worried about Daddy instead of badgering me?"

FB stared at her. "That's liquor talking, isn't it? Avoid reality. Responsibility slides off you, doesn't it? No wonder he plans to give a boost to that rehab center you went to. He probably figures you'll spend a lot of time there."

"Whatever. I was sober a long time afterwards. I don't know why you're venting at me when you should be worried about Daddy."

A tap on the door followed by Franklin's cardiologist entering the waiting room interrupted them.

"Got him comfortable, but he needs a heart transplant soon, very soon."

Anger flashed across FB's face. "He's been on the waiting list for months. Surely a man who's contributed so many millions to this hospital can be next."

Bethany bolted upright. "Heart transplant? What are you talking about? Why can't he have another bypass? Roy, Glenda's husband had…" Bethany said.

FB shook his head and slapped her arm. "Shut up. He didn't want you to know. His heart's been failing." He turned toward the doctor. "So when can this happen?"

"Scheduling isn't the problem. His AB negative blood will cause his body to reject even the universal O donor." The doctor shook his head. "I've contacted national, international and even private facilities to alert me if a match is found."

"But is he, is he going to . . ." Bethany squeezed her eyes shut and sobbed "to die?"

The cardiologist rubbed his balding head. "He's had an episode but right now he's resting." He looked from one to the other. "You both should go home, let him rest. Restrict all visitors and tomorrow stay no longer than ten minutes. He needs rest, understand?"

"Can I see him now, please?" Bethany said.

"Absolutely not. When he rests his heart rests. So go home." With a nod the cardiologist was gone.

On the Uber ride back to the Dunbar Building to get their cars neither Bethany nor FB spoke. As Bethany approached her car, FB grabbed her upper arm and spun her around to face him.

"This is your fault," he said.

***

Torn between worrying about her father's health and thrilled at his generosity, she pressed a cold cloth against her throbbing forehead. The apartment's buzzer sounded, sending Bethany racing toward the door. An android with a flashing screen on its chest stood alongside a package, Bethany searched for her driver's license then remembered the guard waving it as she and FB left for the hospital. She placed her Dunbar ID on the robot's screen. After a beep it turned and shoved a waist-high package into the room.

"Who sent this? I'm waiting for a delivery, but it should be taller" she said.

"Ne.o.dy.nam.ics," the robot answered. Its screen went dark. It turned and left.

"Must have to be assembled," Bethany said. She pulled out the packing materials and screamed. "FB, you slimy bastard."

Reading the accompanying pamphlet her face reddened:

- Plug Heiney, your new robot into an electrical outlet for twenty four hours.
- Place your robot away from liquor serving area. Its sensors are sensitive.

- Scan front and back of driver's license or other photo ID into viewer, found on back.
- To activate the breathalyzer insert a straw into the valve on top.
- Blow into it.
- Within thirty seconds results register in Heiney's viewer, found on back.
- See trouble shooting, page 4, before calling Neodynamics Customer Service.

She smashed a half-filled pitcher against the wall, then kicked the box. It slid several feet away from her. Surprised it was so light, she picked up the robot and stood on the scale with it. She acquired only eight pounds. She slogged down a double shot. The robot's screen lit.

"I'm taking you where you can do some good," she said as she loaded Heiney into the car.

***

Bethany arrived at Kenny's Bar ten minutes before her shift. Pulling the robot behind her she entered shouting and open armed. "Hi everybody. I brought my breathalyzer friend."

Hoots and whistles rose from the customers seated and those playing pool.

From behind the bar Kenny leaned to get a better look. "Get that thing out of here."

"Sorry Kenny." She patted it. "No more DUIs. It's gonna keep me and your customers out of jail."

Customers seated at the bar laughed and elbowed one another.

"Go ahead, laugh. They'll be pulling you over, not me," Bethany said.

The robot's screen lit and it began to beep. Bethany pulled out a straw, waved it like a magician's wand. "Watch this," she yelled and puffed into the robot.

It beeped. Kenny and the customers clustered around and pointed at its display, a .01.

"Damnedest thing I ever saw," Kenny said.

Bethany wedged herself between them and the robot. "Don't get so close. You drunks'll screw up the readings."

Seated back on their barstools, the men talked it over and agreed with Bethany. Heiney could help them all stop drinking in time.

Taking her usual position behind the bar she set up drinks for them.

"What are you going to name your new pet, Bethany?"

Bethany turned her back, bent over and slapped her hip. "They already named it. Heiney."

***

After closing the bar at two A.M. Bethany went to Kenny's apartment. As she slid into bed he woke up. He moved to a chair alongside his nightstand and lit a cigarette.

"My Daddy's really sick, might die," she slurred.

Kenny took a long drag and blew the smoke at her.
"I ain't going with this robot, B, Don't want it in my bar. I got the Twitter and Facebook offers from Neodynamics over a month ago. Can rent it for a hundred bucks a month. Said no."

"But if you'd had it the night Josh and Big Sam got picked up they'd have left before . . ."

He nodded and smashed his cigarette into the overflowing ashtray on the nightstand..

"Exactly. I'm running a business. Don't want them leaving after just one."

"Kenny, just cut the liquor. No big deal," Bethany said.

"Do you think I want the ATF in there?"

"What? Everybody does it. You're talking crazy," she said.

"Is that what you've been doing when I took a break?" Kenny's face grew red as he ground his cigarette into the ashtray.

Bethany looked at the ceiling and did the dumb blond, side to side head wobble.

"Cutting liquor's illegal, Stupid." Kenny lit another cigarette. "I could lose my license." He poured two fingers of Jack Daniels into a glass, took a sip and leaned his head back against his chair.
"Sorry, B, I already decided. It and you have got to go."

"What do you mean, 'go'?" She poured a shot into the dirty glass on the nightstand.

"Just what I said. You come in with your mechanical toy and try to take over my business. I let you work there, drunk. Half the time the register's short. Who do you think you are making decisions for my business?"

"I think I bummed your start-up money from my daddy. That's who I am. Without me there'd be no Kenny's Bar."

"Naw. That's history. You're a thing of my past. Ain't you gone yet?" He shoved her, pushing her toward the bed's edge.

She grabbed the blanket.

"Loser," she said and slept on the couch, dreaming of ways to kill him and her brother. When she woke she found her clothes and cosmetics piled against the couch.

***

Bethany stomped past FB's Alissa, who put up both hands in a "halt" gesture.

"Miss Dunbar, Bethany, please stop. He's in a meeting. He can't be . . ."

Bethany shoved the door so hard it slammed against the wall. She took several steps toward her brother. The four Oriental men seated at the conference table twitched as if they felt a sudden chill. Her fists pushed tight against her waist, Bethany hovered over her brother, seated at the head of the table.

"How dare you, FB. What kind of sick humor sends a beer keg robot?" She held up a picture of R2Beer2. She turned toward the

Oriental men. "That's a Heineken keg with metal paddles for legs and arms. It senses liquor."

FB's customers exchanged glances then, hesitant, leaned toward the picture.

FB nodded toward the men. "My apologies for the interruption." He pushed his chair back, grabbed Bethany's upper arm and shoved her ahead of him toward the front office. Before he could close the conference room door she twisted away from him.

"Let go of me, you oaf," she yelled.

"Gentlemen. I apologize. Please excuse me for a moment," FB said

The men exchanged poker-face glances then studied the contracts resting on the table.

"Call security and get tea and snacks for our guests," FB told Alissa after he closed the conference room door.

Bethany pounded on the secretary's desk. "Alissa, don't go. He doesn't want you to find out how rotten he is," Bethany said loud enough to reach the men in the conference room.

Hands trembling, Alissa grabbed the phone, dialed and hurried out.

Glaring, teeth clenched, FB pushed Bethany into an upholstered chair. "That beer keg robot fits you, you lounge lizard. We've got four hundred orders already from bars world-wide. Kenny should thank me."

"Ha, like you're so great, fair haired child. When Daddy gets out of the hospital…" She said and started to rise.

"Shhh. He swore me to silence," FB said and whispered. "He thinks it's best no one here or any of our customers know he's in the hospital. So button your lip."

"So, get him on the phone. Kenny doesn't like Heiney. I want to talk to Daddy."

Still whispering, FB leaned closer. "You in denial? Didn't you hear his cardiologist yesterday? He's got serious heart problems. I'm not going to let you make things worse."

"So if he dies, I get an equal share of the company, right?" Her eyes narrowed as she shifted in her chair. "You won't tell me to shut up then, will you?"

FB's face reddened. "Yes, and I told him he should give you an allowance through a trust fund. Were you drunk at the meeting? You should get a kick in the ass. Mom'd still be alive if you'd come even half way to simple decency, She'd cry for days about you."

Bethany shook her head. "Hey, don't blame me for her depression, or for her going to two doctors for sleeping pills so she could finish the job. She's better off . . ."

FB lifted his arm and clenched his fist.

She jerked her chin upward. "Bring it. Go ahead. Let's see what Daddy thinks about his Vice President of Sales beating on his hundred pound sister."

FB grabbed her hair and pushed her head back against the chair's cushion. His brows furrowed and eyes narrowed, he leaned butterfly-kisses close. She could smell his Listerine-scented breath.

"You said you wanted a robot to take to your reunion. Your tenth reunion. You and all of them pushing thirty. What'll they talk about? Careers and successful husbands? Their adorable children. You'll have nothing to say, will you?"

"Shut up," Bethany lifted her middle finger.

"Maybe some of them are lounge lizards like you or maybe just drunks. You need to take along a joke to hide how big a joke you are."

Arms waving, Bethany shook her head. He released his grip on her hair. Lowering her head, studying the arm of the chair, tears streamed down her cheeks.

"You were always his favorite," she said, covering her eyes with her hands.

"Favorite? No. I did what I was supposed to do, did what they wanted." FB crossed his arms. "I have to earn my way. You sit on your ass, fall down drunk, never hold a decent job, and you're still Dad's treasure." He paced to the door and back.

"I have a job," Bethany said.

"Right, minimum wage with free drinks. But me?" FB thumped his chest. Dad holds me accountable for every single mistake anybody else makes." FB studied the ceiling then glared at her. "He gives and gives to you, nothing asked in returned. No questions asked."

Bethany lifted one eyebrow. "You can tell yourself that, but you'll never convince me." She stood up. "Get out of my way. Me and my Heiney are going to get drunk."

"What?" FB said as he stepped away from her.

"Heineken Beer Keg Robot R2BEER2, get it stupid," she said, slamming the door.

She watched the lights over the elevator: Fifty, Forty. At thirty the doors slid open and revealed two security guards.

"Miss Dunbar, we got a call," a guard said.

Bethany slid her sleeve upward. "Just look what Vice President of Sales, Franklin Baldwin, Junior, did to me," Red ovals were on her arm, imprinted by FB's fingers.

The guards took deep breaths, eyes widened. They stood, stiffened like frozen. After a long moment one coughed.

"Well, um, we can't really, uh that is, unless you're willing to write up a report . . ."

Bethany glanced at her watch. "That'll make me late for work." She raised her eyebrows and tilted her head. "Report to who?" She looked closer to read the guard's name tag. "McGuire, is it?"

McGuire nodded and the other guard shrugged.

"Right," she said and clapped her hands together. "You'll make photos a part of your report?"

The guards looked at one another.

"Yes Miss Dunbar, we do if a photo seems to be needed."

"All your reports wind up at HR, don't they?"

"No, Miss Dunbar, complaint reports always are reviewed by Mister Dunbar, Senior."

Bethany smiled. "Oh, I see. Then, yes, I do want photos and to report physical abuse and maybe sexual discrimination." She did the 'dumb blond' side-to-side head wobble. "How do you think my father will react?"

***

As Bethany picked up Heiney at Kenny's Bar she banged an empty glass several times against the bar. "I quit. Tonight I'm headed to Secrets. Me and Heiney will be welcome there."

The bar erupted in shouts and laughter.

"You kidding? Old Barney and Kenny have hated one another since . . ."

"Since forever,"

Bethany winked and nodded toward them. "Exactly why I'm taking my business there."

Answering the confused expressions on some of the patrons, a man at the end of the bar shouted, "Yeah Barney beats Kenny every year in the Bloody Mary Contest."

"All the way back to 2038 I think," another one said.

Bethany hit the bar again. "If you come with me, drinks are on me all night. R2BEER2's party. First one to hit 3.0 is the winner."

A mass exit ensued.

At Secrets Bethany showed her corporate credit card to the bartender. "All drinks on me. Give yourself a big tip and I'll have a vodka martini," she said.

Nobody made it to 3.0. Bethany made it to 1.4.

"Last call," the bartender said, handed her the bill, then extinguished the neon Budweiser sign in Secrets' plate glass window.

Bethany signed it, lifted her half-empty glass, rotated it left and right. The bartender stopped wiping the bar and leaned close to her.

"Not happening. You're over your limit," he said, picked up the signed bill and, still wiping the bar, moved away from her.

"I got no limits. My father will . . ."

The bartender crossed his arms over his chest. "Will thank me.

I'm calling a cab for you," He tapped his phone and gave the bar's address. "Ten minutes, tops, Bethany," he said.

Three men at the end of the bar laughed and one of them set a five in front of them.

"She's going to put her head down and pass out," he said.

"Nah, she'll fall off the bar stool. Again," another said and slid a five onto the bar, close to the other one.

"This says she's going to slug the driver when he shows up," the third man said and set his money on the bar.

"Kiss this," Bethany yelled, stumbled as she left her bar stool and slapped her hip.

The three men broke into loud laughing.

"Told you she'd fall off," one said and reached for the three bills in front of them.

"Not so quick. Driver's not here yet and her butt never hit the ground,"

"Taxi? Who called for a cab?" the driver asked as he entered.

"Her," the bartender said and pointed.

Bethany staggered toward the driver and gave him a shove.

"Get the hell out of here," she spit toward him.

Startled, the driver backed away from her. "Hey lady, you think I want a puking drunk in my cab?" He hurried out.

Bethany swayed and sifted through her purse until she found her keys. Turning toward the snickering men she swayed again and dangled her keys overhead.

"See these. They're to my Mer-r-r-chedes. That's a ride you'll never own."

The men who were betting let out whoops and the winner stood up and waved the three bills at her.

"Thanks Bethany,"

She glared, lifted her middle finger and left the bar, shoving R2BEER2 ahead of her. Its digital screen flashed multi-colored lights and made clicking sounds.

***

Bethany found her car by repeatedly pressing its fob. After several fumbling attempts to unlock her car, she slid behind the wheel and slung R2BEER2 into the passenger seat. Its lights and sounds intensified as she pulled away from the curb.

Having a problem staying awake she drove ten miles an hour.

A cruiser pulled behind her.

Bethany pressed the gas pedal, crossed the center line and continued driving in the oncoming lane.

The police car's driver flipped on blue lights.

Instead of pulling over, Bethany floored the gas pedal. The cruiser took off in pursuit. Her Mercedes, faster than the cruiser, lunged forward and outdistanced it.

"Too slow," she laughed, speeding through city streets, ignoring traffic lights, weaving and barely missing parked cars.

The cruiser's driver notified the dispatcher a speeding car was heading for the freeway. A second cruiser positioned at an intersection saw her zoom past, turned on lights and siren.

Distracted, Bethany ignored a red light and T-boned a pickup. The truck drove into a parked car. Bethany's forehead slammed against the steering wheel. Blood splattered the windshield and oozed across the dashboard and onto her clothes.

The policemen in the two cruisers called for ambulances. Before the tow truck left with Bethany's Mercedes a policeman set R2BEER2 on the curb, so he could locate her purse to send with her to the hospital.

The robot's flashing lights and audio sounds intensified. Its screen flashed "1.6. Do not operate machinery."

"Damnedest thing I ever saw," the policeman said as he joined his partner in the cruiser.

"You leaving it there, on the curb?" his partner asked.

"What? You want that alien thing in here with us?" His partner shook his head and started the cruiser.

They followed the ambulances as they rushed Bethany and the other driver to the closest hospital. At the Emergency entrance the policeman handed Bethany's purse to the clerk.

Searching through it she found Bethany's corporate ID. After scanning its bar code she sent a message to FB's phone, imprinted within ID. When FB arrived an hour later, the clerk referred him to Intensive Care.

"Bethany Dunbar. What room is she in? How is she? Why isn't she in surgery?" He startled the nurse at the monitor-filled desk. She leaned toward the fifth monitor and studied its screen.

"Dr. Wooleridge, reviewed her CT scan and decided he would need the family's permission. He said surgery would be risky." She hesitated. "And possibly unnecessary."

"Tell me exactly where I can find her," FB said in the tone he used with his employees. The nurse stepped back from him.

"She's right across the hall. But you have to wait. They're in there to…"

FB ignored her. He became aware of mechanical pulsing and wheezing sounds. Two people dressed in green scrubs adjusted settings on suspended bags of liquids. From the doorway he could see the peaks and valleys of the heart monitor. Another monitor on the other side of the bed showed a wavy line slightly lifting and falling. This was the monitor the people in scrubs looked at frequently as they adjusted tubes attached to her. Drawing close to her he turned toward one of the nurses.

"I'm her brother. How bad is it?"

She shrugged and pointed to the wavy lines on the screen. "Brain waves are weak." She pointed at the heart monitor. "Her heart's strong. No sign of shock, yet," the nurse said.

"What does that mean? Where's the neurologist. Tell him to fix this. Our father can't withstand losing…"

"He's seen her, sir. Head injuries surprise us both ways. Sometimes a miracle, sometimes, well, not always good news. Please go to the waiting room. The doctor will come there and talk with you"

FB stared at Bethany's swollen cranium and blackened eyes.

"She was so pretty." he said as he left. "I meant is so pretty," he called to the nurses.

Passing the nurses' station on his way to the waiting room a voice called his name.

"Yes?" He looked around. A woman holding a plastic bag stood up inside the nurses' station.

"Mr. Dunbar, would you like to put Miss Dunbar's belongings in a locker?"

"Belongings?"

"Yes sir, her clothes and the purse a policeman found in the car."

"Oh yes, I would. Thank you," he said, remembering Bethany had a corporate credit card. He took the bag, found Bethany's wallet containing her Neodynamics credit card.

"Please put these in a locker for her," he said and handed the plastic bag containing Bethany's clothes, shoes and purse. He found his way to the men's restroom, rinsed her blood off the credit card and off his hands.

Returning to the waiting room he found several tearful women. He picked up a sailing magazine and found an article describing how to refurbish an old craft. The doctor's voice startled him.

"Mr. Dunbar, would you join me where we can speak privately?" FB followed him. The doctor, accompanied by a tall woman, sat alongside him at a small table with a laptop between them. He pulled up a graph with Bethany's name at the top.

"Your sister's brain shows little activity. We think she was not secured by her seatbelt. We know her forehead hit the steering wheel. But it appears her head snapped backward and damaged her medulla. In addition her blood is not congealing normally because of the volume of alcohol she consumed," the doctor said.

FB stared at the graph. Its line sloped toward the bottom of the monitor.

"Does she have a living will, Mr. Dunbar? The tall woman asked.

FB shook his head. "Don't know. Probably not. She's only twenty-eight."

The woman nodded. "We were unable to find her driver's license. Do you know if she signed her organ donor authorization on her license? If all fails, she can save another life or lives if she agreed to donate her organs,"

FB stared at the floor.

"We realize this is a very painful moment for you, Mr. Dunbar, but saving another is very likely within your sister's future."

FB's father's last conversation echoed:

> "The heart grafts they put in five years ago failed. They tell me I need a transplant. Not too likely to match me. AB-negative blood isn't…." Franklin had drawn a deep breath and closed his eyes. "Promise me you'll take care of Bethany. She's so like her mother, so small, so tormented by alcohol, drugs and . . ."
>
> "Sure. okay, Dad. Just take care of yourself. If there's a heart here or anywhere in the world I'll find it for you," FB said and blinked away tears.

"Doctor, can you tell me what blood type Bethany has? My father is AB negative and . . ."

The doctor searched through the laptop resting on the table. "Here's her X-ray and CT Scan. The neurologist has not recommended surgery. She's not stable enough to survive it." The doctor continued reading. He looked at FB and took a deep breath. "Any reason you're asking blood type?"

"I hate to even think this." He lifted his shoulders and released a loud sigh. "But my father needs a heart. You see, my father is next for a transplant but his rare blood type . . ." FB studied the ceiling then gritted his teeth. "Doctor, I may lose my whole family right here, right now. If one could save the other . . ."

"AB-negative. That's her blood type. But the nurses couldn't find her driver's license with her organ donor authorization on the back. We need to see if she signed to donate her organs. Without that..." the doctor shrugged and shook his head.

He left as FB phoned his wife, Barb, and relayed Bethany's condition and the inheritance conversation that triggered his father's heart into distress.

"They've asked if she signed to donate her organs. I think if something happens to Bethany my Dad may receive her heart. Her blood type matches his," FB said.

Barb's gasp at the other end of the phone clued FB she had more to say.

"What are you thinking?" He asked, dreading her logic.

"He's giving a million to the rehab center? They didn't help her, did they?" Barb said.

"No, I don't think they helped her. But, yes that's what he's done. If she dies, I think it'll kill him," FB said.

"Then what happens to her half of the corporation?" his wife said.

"Barb, what kind of a question . . .?

"You've worked too hard for you miss out. Does she have a will? You could wind up with Kenny as half owner of Neodynamics."

"Barb, you're so cold." FB rubbed his cheek, noticing he needed a shave.

"Hey I'm a financial planner. That's my job, remember?" she said.

"Well Dad didn't ask you, did he?" FB shifted in his chair.

"No, if he had, I'd have reminded him how much you've contributed to his wealth."

"I mentioned that to him. He said he thinks I've been paid well all along."

"Yes and you've been a great son. The way I see it you lose whether she recovers or not," Barb said.

"What do you mean, Barb, 'whether or not?'"

"Okay, if she lives she gets half plus equal voice in the company. If she's sick, she'll drain everything dry and leave you out in the cold," she said.

Narrowing his eyes he thought about his wife's conclusions.

"FB, are you still there?" Barb said.

"Um huh, I'm thinking."

"There's another possibility. If she passes and her heart replaces his you can be sure he's likely to spend, spend, spend setting up endowments and Lord knows what else in her name."

Squeezing his eyes shut tight, FB tapped his fingers on the table.

"So all you see is me coming out losers after all I've done for both of them, is that it?" FB said.

"You've got it. He's spoiled her and showered her with way more than he's given you. He won't change that. He's always expected you to earn your way. That won't change. But either way she may bankrupt the company."

"We're talking about my father, Barb." FB punched the off button on his phone. He blinked back tears as his nose dripped. Searching for a handkerchief, his hand touched Bethany's driver license in his pocket. *The first floor guard. He had it. I took her license from the guard.*

He stood and with his hand on the doorknob and hesitated. *Barb's right. If she lives he'll spend millions trying to make her well. I'll watch all I worked for dissolve out from under me. If she dies, gives him her heart, he'll spend millions being grateful to that damned rehab center or memorializing her name through endowments.*

FB found his way to a restroom. Inside a stall he withdrew the license and gasped when he turned it over. Her signature indicated she had agreed to be an organ donor.

"Too many bad choices. Too little too late," he said and slid her driver's license back into his pocket.

A RIVER ASSAILED

By *Jan Werff*

The social compact is broken. The American way is on life-support, and free men must fend for themselves.

The alarm on Birdsong's watch peeped, and both mean awoke instantly. The moon was a sliver far down the western horizon. They broke fast in darkness on energy bars and trail mix and cold water from the canteen. There was no fire to mark their spot, and no coffee to cause a hand tremor later.

At last Birdsong spoke. "We ready to do this thing?"

"Almost. Take this," Lightfoot replied.

By feel Birdsong knew what was pressed into his hand. It was two claws of a Grizzly bear strung on fishing line separated by a single bead and framed by two more beads. Lightfoot had come upon the bear that spring. Was he more surprised to see a griz that early in the season, or was the bear more surprised at the speed with which Lightfoot unslung his rifle and fired? Birdsong had seen the tanned hide hanging over an entire wall of Lightfoot's lodge, a single .308 caliber hole centered between the animal's eyes.

Birdsong slipped the fish line loop over his head and buttoned it inside his camo jacket. Among Northern Plains Indians, the presentation of such a talisman was not insignificant.

Silently they loaded the canoe. The packs, solid and squat, went in first. Then the sleeping bags, a bow and quiver of arrows, and a Ruger Mini-14 Lightfoot picked up at a gun show in Billings six years earlier. The rifle was old and cold, and Lightfoot had worn gloves to polish the cartridges with

Windex before loading the magazine. There would be no comebacks should he have to use it and later lose it.

There was no fishing gear. The fish weren't biting on that stretch of the river that day, and maybe never again. The state's Department of Natural Resources (DNR) spokesperson blamed the massive fish kill on a microscopic parasite that attacked the kidneys of fish. The parasite, though very rare, flourished in warm shallow waters. This despite rainfall being above normal that season.

This was the same DNR rep who had shared the rostrum with the politicians who brayed 'JOBS, JOBS, JOBS' when announcing that oil companies would use hydraulic fracturing techniques to pry oil and gas reserves from shale a few miles north of the river.

There was little fall out for the politicians. Fish don't vote, and the handful of fishing guides and subsistence fishermen downstream was too small a constituency to matter. So long as the kill didn't affect the tourism related to the parks two hundred miles downstream there shouldn't be a problem.

And there were jobs. Truck drivers from all over the country poured in to collect the high wages, and skilled workers from all over the oil patch arrived to share in the bonanza. There was not so much work for locals, and the prices at the Wal-Mart soared.

The independent labs in Missouri and Kansas that Birdsong and Lightfoot had visited cited another possible cause for the fish kill – high concentrations of BTEX in both the river water and soil. BTEX, composed mainly of benzene, toluene, ethyl benzene and xylene, along with a cocktail of other toxins and heavy metals, was the main ingredient in the hydraulic fracturing fluid that was injected under pressure into the shale substrate.

With the bust in the world oil market, it was no longer economical to ship the waste BTEX by rail to a treatment and recycling facility. It was much more efficient to dump the toxic waste in the river.

They slipped the canoe into the stream and paddled in near silence upstream. Birdsong could hear the paddle blades pulling through the water but little else. The ash forest was quiet at that hour, and animals had stopped drinking on this stretch of the river. How Lightfoot navigated in the darkness was a mystery to Birdsong, perhaps by smell. There was a distinct chemical odor on the water. There was little danger of being seen — the oil company's security was at the drill site — and if they were seen they were just two Indian dudes hunting or camping or whatever they do.

Northern Plains Indians are warriors. It's in their blood and bones. In the military they often volunteered for the most hazardous assignments. Birdsong and Lightfoot joined up together and trained together. After graduation from boot camp they'd drawn different schools for advanced training, though both had eventually been assigned to the Third Battalion of the Sixth Marine Regiment. The "Teufelshunden," Hounds from Hell, so named for their fighting spirit by German troops at Belleau Wood over a hundred years ago. Not much has changed since. Lightfoot had served two tours as a scout/sniper. Birdsong served two tours as a combat engineer.

"Birdsong, clear that minefield."

"Yes, sir."

"Birdsong, disarm that IED."

"Yes, sir."

"Birdsong, blow that bridge."

"Yes, sir."

In the narrow gorges and passes of the Afghan mountains there'd been sufficient bridges and rock formation to blow that he'd become something of an artist with the C-4 plastic explosive.

On the trip back from the Missouri and Kansas laboratories they'd made a late-night visit to the storage building of a quarry in Minnesota, picking up a hundred pounds of Birdsong's art supplies.

There was nothing to gain by attacking the drills, pumps and derricks. They were plentiful and such an attack would accomplish nothing. The key to stopping the hydraulic fracturing was to make it unprofitable. The best way to do that, Birdsong figured, was to make the transport of the oil to the refineries in Illinois prohibitively expensive. There was no pipeline, and just a two-lane road serviced the drill site. The oil went out in trains of tank cars along a long disused, but now refurbished, spur down to the main rail line and then east.

No one should get hurt.

There is a line between immoral and illegal Birdsong didn't want to cross. The chemical pollutant the oil company dumped into the river was a legal act, an unfortunate accident, if the dumping was discovered. The government had granted permits to exploit the mineral wealth of the land, though the dumping was certainly immoral.

Birdsong had killed before – an act of war the government called it, so legal. He'd blown a bridge with a convoy of trucks crossing. The trucks and thirty-six souls had gone into the gorge. None had come out. To the Afghani, Birdsong was the interloper, the foreigner, the terrorist. To them his act was both illegal and immoral. It was a matter of perspective.

Lightfoot never spoke of his war. After his discharge, he reverted to being a man of the land, living a quiet life, sometimes in a Tipi in good weather.

He was less complicated than Birdsong, but once he'd consulted the spirits, nothing would dissuade him from his course of action.

Lightfoot:

America invades a smaller, much weaker country to secure

a source to feed America's thirst for oil.

Might makes right. It's the American way.

Mexican drug cartels buy major governmental influence with the profits made on America's insatiable craving for drugs.

Birds fly. Fish swim. Politicians take.

An oil conglomerate poisons a pristine wild river to preserve its profit margin.

Not within reach of my arm.

In an hour of steady paddling, a darker shadow loomed over the stygian aura of the river. Lightfoot steered the canoe toward the south bank directly under the bridge. The bow grated against the sandy bottom, and Birdsong hopped into the water and hauled the canoe up the bank.

They'd gone over the plan enough times that there was no need to speak.

The bridge was of the Pennsylvania Truss variety, two steel spans resting on steel supports which in turn rested atop three stone block piers. Birdsong had shot pictures with his cell phone on a previous scouting trip, and knew the center pier in mid-stream was the best point of attack.

Lightfoot and Birdsong humped the packs out to the center of the bridge, making three trips each to transfer all the equipment. Birdsong climbed down onto the pier, and Lightfoot handed the packs down one at a time.

Then Lightfoot picked out the pair of red-lensed lanterns. He was to run the lanterns about a mile in each direction up and down the track. Trains of empty tank cars usually arrived around ten a.m. and departed with loaded cars around one p.m., but Birdsong had insisted on the precaution, knowing any approaching train would stop at the sight of a red lantern. By the time the ruse was discovered, Lightfoot and Birdsong would be well away.

While Lightfoot did that, Birdsong would make preparations to blow the bridge. He had a small headset light. Security was one thing, but handling C-4 and blasting caps in total darkness was another. He knew in advance that the pier was granite, a tough, durable stone that had neither fracture nor cleavage properties to aid in breaking. The pictures he'd taken gave him a fair idea of how the stones had been joined and where the larger of the natural cracks in the stone were, and so he'd been able to pre-shape fifty pounds of explosive to blast straight down.

The remaining fifty pounds he'd shaped to blast upward and outward against the lower chord members of the truss. These horizontal steel members added strength and kept the vertical beams of the truss from buckling. With the chord beams eliminated, the bridge would collapse under its own weight. Birdsong set the charges and fused them and turned off his headlight. As he was doing so, Lightfoot ran past to set the second red lantern.

Birdsong began inflating a child's plastic swimming pool with a canister of compressed gas. He arranged the pool squarely atop the downward blasting charge on the pier. Nothing helps tamp a shaped charge as well as water. He heard Lightfoot scrambling down the bank as he lowered the hand operated water pump attached to thirty feet of green garden hose. Pumping forty-five gallons of water up to the pool would be the most time-consuming aspect of the plan.

Just as they prepared to depart, Lightfoot dropped a couple of Greenpeace brochures in the brush. That would be a bone the FBI could chew on when the investigation began. And there would be an investigation. By noon the news networks would have aerial photography of the bridge collapsed in the river. The EPA would be forced to act.

As for Greenpeace, they'd relish the attention and sic a platoon of lawyers on the FBI and EPA. When Birdsong was satisfied that all was ready, he connected both charges to the pre-paid, and untraceable, cell phone they'd bought at a Target store. It was a trigger just like any one of the hundred or so such devices he'd disarmed in Afghanistan. It was very convenient that the oil company had installed its own cell tower to support the drill site.

Big business being big business, it seemed likely the railroad's insurer would balk at rebuilding the bridge, possibly keeping the issue in court for many years. Also, it seemed likely the railroad would continue charging rental on the rail cars and locomotives trapped north of the river, making the oilfield that much less profitable.

False dawn cast the bridge in silhouette as they paddled downstream. Birdsong sat facing upstream, watching for any activity on the bridge. As they reached the bend in the river they stopped and Birdsong took a last look at the bridge before punching the speed dial.

Sound travels faster through water than air, so they heard one explosion followed shortly by a second. As pairs of vertical members broke free of the superstructure, sharp twanging snaps punctuated a long, metallic groan. The mid-stream ends of the twin spans settled slowly toward the river bottom.

Satisfied they paddled away.

The End

THE OFFICIAL BEGINNER'S GUIDE TO THE MID-LIFE CRISIS

By *Jan Werff*

Chapter One: Go With the Flow

Going through the mid-life crisis is as natural to the American male as watching Sunday sports on TV, and not only is it survivable, but also it is possible to emerge on the other side as a better, stronger man. Of course there are steps to be taken and a few simple rules, sign posts really, to help you on the journey. The first rule being, Go With the Flow.

It is the constant struggle, the rebellion, against the slings and arrows of outrageous fortune which makes the whole process stressful. When embracing the change, treating it as an adventure, will carry you through to a brighter tomorrow.

I had a pretty good time with my mid-life crisis, all things considered, and you can too.

I think of mine as a second childhood and fondly remember the day I turned the corner and embraced the flow. I was walking in the back drive of the office campus as was my habit since my wife kicked me out six weeks previous. Daily, at lunch time, I'd walk to the cafeteria and pick up a salad, walk it back to my desk, change into sneakers, and go striding out along the quiet streets of the office park. I did this faithfully each noon and again in the evening. The exercise combined with a cessation of tobacco and alcohol had had a notable effect on my body, and I was starting to smart less from the upcoming divorce.

Tall, willowy and strawberry blond, she wore a green skirted suit and high heels that sank into the soft asphalt of the parking lot as her interception course closed. As she got closer I could see she was a bit older than I had guessed from a distance, maybe thirty-seven, with a hint of sun lines around the eyes, but nonetheless attractive for all that. And best of all, no wedding ring.

Since the wife, I'd had almost no human contact outside of work, and no romantic contact at all, and it seemed like a long time.

"Do you mind if I tag along? I like to exercise during lunch, but I hate to do it alone," she said.

Our company, Quasar Petrochemical, encouraged employee fitness, and of the several hundred employees on campus a good many were seen walking outside on nice days and through the tunnels between the buildings when the weather turned inclement. The chances that the lady was alone other than by choice, coupled with the stiletto heels she wore, let me think her story was less than the whole truth. Still I was flattered, because up until that moment the opposite sex had shown little interest in me, and attractive females none at all.

"By all means," I said.

I normally walked between two and three miles at lunch, but we'd gone less than a hundred yards when it became apparent that she'd never make such a distance in her heels.

As we approached one of the many picnic tables arranged under shade trees around the campus, I suggested we cut our walk short and just visit, a suggestion she accepted.

Her name was Debby Hart. Debby was a fine name for a young girl or even a brand of snack cake, but struck me as odd in a grown woman.

"Debby, short for Deborah? In Hebrew, Deborah means prophetess," I said.

"Oh, are you Jewish?"

It sounded like it could be an important question. Unsure which path to take, I opted for the truth.

"What? Oh, no, lapsed Catholic. I work in communications and possess a wealth of useless knowledge such as biblical meanings of names."

In fact, in my non-svelte life, I had plenty of lonely evenings to read the Encyclopedia Britannia, Webster's and the dictionary of synonyms and antonyms.

She worked in the order processing department (the OPD), entering and tracking orders as they arrived via e-mail from the outside sales reps, and following up with customers. One of several facts I gleaned about her in that visit, which by necessity she cut at twenty minutes due to the women of OPD being on a strict schedule for arrivals and departures. But she did promise to meet me that evening at the Silver Stream House, the company watering hole.

The Silver Stream House was voted by the readers of Cincinnatian Magazine as the number one place to meet cougars, that most elusive solitary huntress of the mating ritual. She was waiting in the parking lot.

"Oh, is this your car?"

I surveyed my forlorn wheels, the standard four, none of which, even when new, could be accused of style. The doors, again four, where faded and oft dinged by shopping carts and the other wears and tears of eleven years of daily use.

"This is it. Good old Brutus, my boon companion lo these many years."

"And it has a name. How nice."

I could see I had failed to impress. And it's not like I was out of practice. I'd never had the ability.

She said, "I'm sorry; I don't have a lot of time. It's my day to car pool after swim practice."

What thirty-something suburban woman isn't going to have kids in an extracurricular activity and a car pool? It's de rigueur.

"No problem," I said, though I had hoped for a little alone time.

"But I do want to see you, maybe later. Let me have your address."

"I told her where I lived, nearby in a single's complex named Harper's Crossing, but known to snide locals as Herpes Crossing, for the abundance of cougars in residence there. She wrote the information on a dollar bill, which I thought odd but insignificant. She put the bill in her wallet, climbed into her car and was gone.

My momentary elation quickly turned to panic. It had been years since I'd entertained a single female at home. And my home barely qualified —a one bedroom apartment with cheap shag carpet, hollow core doors and eggshell paint job. Coupled with no furniture, an empty refrigerator, and bed sheets serving as curtains, it screamed "going through a divorce." It screamed loser.

I took a deep breath, cleared my head a bit and hopped in my car. I made a beeline for the Kroger Marketplace located near my complex. I sanitized a cart and hustled to the deli. I grabbed a half shrimp ring, a pre-cut cheese tray and a veggie platter, dip included. I got a twelve pack of imported beer, though I'd been on the wagon for six weeks, a bottle of red, a bottle of white and a tube of plastic stemware. I snagged a pack of Chinette plates and a container of assorted plastic flatware, paying a few cents extra to get the "nice" ones.

Then I was off to the apartment to impose order in the time allotted.

Luckily, I hadn't lived there long enough for the bathroom to be too gross, so a quick wipe down with that morning's damp bath towel, which was conveniently located on the floor, sufficed.

I owned a vacuum, the soon-to-be ex-wife's old one, which I ran around the carpet enough to leave wheel tracks, evidence that I was not a total slob, and then rearranged my living room furniture.

I put both woven plastic mesh lawn chairs in front of my nineteen-inch portable TV, tuned the boom box to soft rock hits of the '80s and '90s, and dashed to the bedroom where my one real piece of furniture, a four poster waterbed, also left over from the '80s and '90s, needed making.

About seven thirty there was a knock on the door. It was she, wearing spandex bicycle shorts, halter top and sneakers.

"I'm on the way home from the gym," she said as she stepped in and shut the door behind her. "We don't have a lot of time. I have to be home before the kid's bedtime," she added as she snaked her arms around my neck.

"Would you care for something to eat or drink?"

"Don't be coy," she said, steering me towards the bedroom.

The waterbed, while incomparable for sleeping, was overrated for sex, in particular for active and athletic sex.

More than once in the next thirty minutes the waves were breaking one way and the bodies going another. Once, during a gymnastic reverse cowgirl position, Debby was unseated and wound up on the floor.

Still, for any faults the session had, breaking my celibate streak was a blessing. And not to look a gift horse in the mouth, so to speak, I had a chance to examine my new playmate's body closely.

Obviously she worked out. She had muscle toned abs and legs, but time had not been kind. She'd gotten heavy stretch marks at some point, presumably during a pregnancy as they were generally located on her stomach. Her butt was nearly flat. Also, my main criticism, she could stand to work a couple Kegels in between sets on the Stairmaster.

Her aerobics were fine. We languored in post coital cuddle just a couple minutes before she was up and in the shower, dried, dressed and out the door. A reverse wham, bam thank-you ma'am, but I'm not complaining.

Though I did notice, to my chagrin, that the cap threads on the water mattress had stripped out, and the mattress now leaked. I could pack the frame with my bath towels, both of them threadbare rejects that even the soon-to-be ex-wife thought were of no value and hence had bequeathed to me.

So that night I slept well in a modified fetal position that kept my feet out of the wet spot.

By morning, of course, the sheet had sopped up half a mattress load, no big deal. I flipped the sheet over the shower curtain rod to dry and formed a plan to purchase a roll of the bachelor's best friend – duct tape.

***

The impending divorce made some positive changes on my work. After I quit boozing, I was a lot sharper in the mornings, and because my new apartment was much closer to the office than the marital home had been, I tended to arrive earlier. Often I was the first person in the office, not that Communications Director Paul S. von Klug would acknowledge it.

He noticed of course, but was far too much an old school Prussian to acknowledge the improvements. His nose was still out of joint because I'd gotten the job. A hustling newspaper reporter with a crappy degree from a land grant college was breathing the same rarefied air as the Big Ten and Ivy League pricks who dominated the company.

His great-grandfather's brother had been some kind of big-deal tank commander in the German army back in the big one. Not a Nazi, he was exonerated at Nuremburg, as von Klug pointed out whenever the topic of family pedigrees was broached. But seventy-five years later von Klug still lived in that historic shadow.

He had the look, the skin drawn tight over the skull, cheekbones and nose. All that was missing was the dueling scar and the monocle to complete a flesh and blood portrait of Rocky and Bullwinkle's Fearless Leader – a name I sometimes referred to him as after a couple pops at the Silver Stream House.

Sometimes after a couple more pops, he'd wax nostalgic. "If the war had gone the other way, my life sure would have been different."

Not that his life wasn't working out. He had the big salary and perks and was the odds on favorite to move into the vice president slot when old Joe Havoline retired.

Yes, von Klug hated me and would've fired me in a minute, except I had a secret.

He's an egomaniacal prick. That's not a secret. And though I'm the writer and editor of a number of customer-based newsletters, the "important" copywriting he farms out to buddies at business-to-business ad agencies.

They had camera-ready art for a new six-color placement for Ultrathene, the company's premiere line of polymer sealants. The premise was old hat, a hand taking a book off a shelf with the caption being "Number One Best Sealer." What a yawn, been done to death, and beneath notice except for the fact that the product name, "Ultrathene," was misspelled on the book's binding.

So von Klug, the ad rep and von Klug's toady, Del, were congratulating themselves on the scintillating ad work, and I was in the background hemming and hawing whether to break the news, or to let it go to press as is and let the fertilizer hit the Cuisinart, so to speak.

So finally, knowing I'd make no friends, I asked, "Has Legal seen this?"

"Of course Legal has seen this. And Sales and Marketing and Division Management," von Klug snarled.

I'd done my duty. Let the fertilizer fly! Not that any would stick to Paul S. von Klug, but perhaps the toady would get some brown on somewhere other than his nose. My spirits lifted; I broke for my luncheon walk while the smart guys headed out to the Silver Stream House for celebratory light beers and sandwiches.

I think of myself as a cork, riding a little higher in the human effluent than some of the other floaters. An effluent whose exact nature and consistency is best left undefined. So I made way per usual, to the company cafeteria for a takeout salad and diet Coke, and then to my office. I dropped my salad off, put my sneaks on, and went for my walk.

Lately I've been dropping into the company health center evenings for a light work out on the machines, mostly the manly ones –bench press, lat pull down and rowing. Although looking in the mirror I tend to see the same old fatty that was getting divorced. Lately some of the women who frequent the club have been giving me the cursory once over, which I considered progress.

When I got back from my walk there was an e-mail, cryptic, but given company cyber security policy, understandable —"tonight, your apartment, 8 PM." It was from D, and I had nothing better to do, so after a stop at the grocery, where I got a small roll of duct tape for a somewhat inflated price, I was home awaiting my booty call.

When she arrived, she was through the door and in my arms in the same instant. The Kohl's shopping bags she carried hit the rug and she wrapped her legs around my waist like kids do in the popular cinema. I don't know what she was thinking, because three times weekly work out or not, she weighed a hundred thirty pounds and we were soon on the living room carpet flinging clothes hither and yon. My ardor rose quickly and in a twinkling I had her on her back and entered and was hanging on for the short, fierce ride that was sex with Debby.

I felt a bit like a rodeo rider lying in a sweat on the floor watching the ceiling fan go round. I could feel the rug burns on my knees and was sure they were bloody, but felt no need to examine them at that time.

I caught my breath, and dutiful host that I am, made an offer. "Would you like a drink or something to nibble on?"

"I'd nibble you if I had the time. But I got to get home, get the kids' homework checked and get them to bed." She had a lascivious grin and a slight overbite I found sexy. I'm told men think slight overbites are sexy because it implies the female's talent for oral sex, although I've had no opportunity to explore this aspect with my hit-and-run serial sexer.

She snatched up one of the shopping bags as she headed for my bathroom.

"I brought you a present. I don't know how you can live like this."

The present was towels and washcloths and a color coordinated toilet tank cover and a little matching carpet. As she walked away, I noticed she had a fresh carpet burn on her back about midway between her shoulders and buttocks.

She hit the shower and turned the whole primping thing around in four minutes flat, a new indoor women's record.

She pecked my cheek. "I'll call you," she said as the door shut behind her.

I don't know why, but it bothered me a little that I didn't know her phone number or where she lived. She wasn't in the book, but a lot of women weren't. It bothered me a little more that it didn't bother me that much. I wondered if I was getting jaded in my dotage.

Nothing seemed to bother me that much anymore. The job was going nowhere. It paid a decent wage as most big companies do, but I was definitely plateaued, and try finding another even vaguely journalistic job at my age. I might as well start writing novels and screenplays, for goodness sake.

The soon-to-be ex-wife's imminent raking of me through court over child support meant I'd have even less, so perhaps that's why I embraced the midlife crisis so cavalierly, so enthusiastically.

In any case the tape job on the waterbed valve slowed the seepage to an acceptable level, and once again in a modified fetal position, I slept the sleep of the righteous.

***

The rug burns on my knees were indeed bloody but scabbing over the next day. If I'd owned a box of Band-Aids, I'd probably have made the effort, futile as it likely would have been on articulating joints, but instead I opted for my oldest brown suit and was off to the office with the sun.

I'd gotten in the habit of starting the coffee pots to dripping when I got in, and working in my office with only the computer screen for light. This was a habit that annoyed von Klug no end, as it was some sort of company code that if you were in your office the ceiling light should be on. Old von Klug had many such little rules that I broke, not out of spite as much as they seemed trivial and something I never thought much about.

In my past life as a reporter, keeping one's trousers zipped was the extent of office protocol, and in my defense, I really didn't know any better.

That morning I was finishing up a long piece on the feared imminent shortage of titanium dioxide, a chemical that makes plastics bright white. The point was to prepare the twenty percent of our customers who represented eighty percent of our sales for a shocking price increase. The other eighty percent of our client base would face rationing.

As it was a corporate piece, I extolled the beauty of blue and yellow picnic coolers and even solid blue and solid red. I was lying, and the customers knew it. Later, I would process photos in my darkroom for the Legal Department —seventy-two frames of the same fifty-pound sack of polyethylene pellets, each frame shot under slightly different lighting conditions.

I loved my dark room. It was cool and soundproof, and it was totally forbidden for anyone to open the lightproof door if the red "occupied" lamp was lit. Since the advent of the digital age, I no longer used film, but this was one time tradition was in my favor. I could work in my boxer shorts or pajamas if I chose, although I didn't. Still, it was nice to have the luxury of freedom in a twelve-foot-square cube.

When I returned to the office, the cryptic e-mail of the day awaited. A change of pace today, instead of a time at my apartment, there was a time and an address: 12225 North Vine St., 6PM.

A road trip? Sex in a location to be announced? Well, alright, I suppose. I wondered if I was experiencing a diminishing marginal return effect on Debby that economists and doctors speak of.

What man feasting on burgers each day doesn't hanker for steak? And what daily steak eater doesn't pine for lobster or even the occasional pork chop?

Still, as soon as office hours concluded I made the journey, and to my surprise, the location was not so much a remote love nest as an automobile dealership.

She was there already, with Mike, a salesman with a red golf shirt stretched over a big gut and an elaborate comb over that waved in the slight breeze.

The deal was set; my eleven-year old Impala plus seventeen thousand dollars in exchange for a five-year-old, Synergy Green and black Chevy Camaro. All I needed to do was sign the credit application, the back of my car title, pass a credit check and the deal was done.

It made sense in a way. Once the child support decree became part of the official record, there is no way I'd qualify for the loan. C'est la vie, I suppose. It was a handsome car with low mileage. It was coming off a lease, and the lessee was a female owner of a dress shop in the mall. References available on request, Mike assured me.

So with more enthusiasm than I really felt I, signed on the dotted line, shook Mike's hand, and was the owner of a sports car.

"But wait, there's more," Debby said as she slid into the passenger seat.

She directed me a few blocks west to a second tier strip mall, and I parked in the back row in the lot of a men's discount clothier.

"Whoa, whoa my little pork chop. I've already run through my allowance for the week."

"Pork chop? What an awful pet name," Debby said. "Besides they're having a BOGO sale. And it's my treat."

She led me into the store, and though the wares on offer would never be mistaken for Armani or Ralph Lauren; they were as nice as anything I owned, and the lady was paying.

Frank, our salesman, quickly assessed my size and in no time was showing me a charcoal gray, three-button suit with a tiny red pinstripe, and as a lagniappe, a lighter gray, double breasted suit, which if one were to squint might be mistaken for Armani.

Frank was also fast with a half dozen light blue long sleeve shirts, buy three get three, and a brace of silk/poly-blend neckties.

And while the tailor took my inseam and chest, I'm nearly a perfect forty-two regular he informed me, Debby went to the sales desk to settle up.

In a trice Frank returned.

"Your alterations will be completed by Tuesday, Mr. Hart. Will that be OK?

"Mr. Hart, oh I'm not . . ."

"Tuesday will be fine," Debby cut me off.

So back in the car I said, "Thank you for the suits. You shouldn't have." I knew that once the alteration started the die was cast.

She tucked the claim check in my shirt pocket.

"Happy to do it. Honestly your wardrobe . . ."

"So now what?" I pondered.

"No time for that today. My God, you are insatiable. Take me back to my car. It's my day to carpool."

So I dropped her at her car and drove home, thinking every mile of the way: "There is no way I can afford this car."

I parked in my assigned spot and hoped that no one dented it overnight. I had the buyer's remorse times three, and was going to rescind my contract and get my Impala back first thing in the morning, which was my right under Ohio law.

Still I slept fitfully that night, couldn't get comfortable in any position. The cap was leaking on the mattress again, and naturally my feet were wet and I dreamed of being lost at sea.

In the morning I rose, shaved and dressed, then hustled to work. Though there was no getting out of the weekly staff meeting short of a bona fide medical emergency.

At least there was pastry and coffee to help the droning of von Klug and his toady pass. But on that day, thank God it was Friday, a technical writer, Rhea, had an announcement of her own.

Rhea belonged to every rinky-dink editor society under the sun. It is her habit to enter every publication she was remotely connected with in the competitions of said editor's societies. And given the budgets Quasar plays with, shoddy spelling notwithstanding, she frequently wins.

This time the award was for technical writing, a how-to booklet on let-down ratio in forming polyethylene bottles, written by a scientist at the Clinton, Iowa, plant, and entrusted to Rhea to get printed.

Why would I care? I don't, except that I am expected to do a publicity blurb for release to the local media and take a new publicity shot. The plagiarism I could care less about, though I've worked at newspapers where that was a firing offense. But getting a presentable photo of the egregious Rhea would involve the whole morning and every trick of the photographer's trade.

Rhea was five-by-five feet of self-absorption –twenty-five cubic feet of bad attitude that I seldom interacted with, except on days like today, when publicizing her capers was a matter of official duty.

So I rushed to my studio and set the side lights to the most flattering angle. I used the no-color straw and powder blue gels in the Fresnel spots to try and put some life in her cadaverous features and smeared a little Vaseline around the edge of the lens. I pulled out all the stops in a futile attempt to make a silk purse out of a horse's rear end.

My morning was consumed.

When I did get to call on the automobile dealership, it was too late. Poor old Brutus, my boon companion of eleven years, had already been compacted.

Like it or lump it. I was the owner of a Synergy Green Chevy Camaro.

The cryptic e-mail du jour arrived after my luncheon walk. Again a new location, a restaurant/bar called the Crown Prince over in Evendale, which I had seen but never been in. Alright I suppose, though I felt like Debby and I should have the talk, redefine our relationship. And today was as good a day as any.

The Crown Prince was behind a strip mall cheek-by-jowl with a commercial butcher shop. The interior was dark, and the air suffused with scofflaw cigarette smoke. Exactly the sort of place you'd come if you didn't want to be seen by anyone you work with, or anyone at all for that matter.

She was there, waiting, behind a frosty bottle of Miller Lite. Though I'd been off the sauce for a six weeks, I said "the same" when our waitress stopped by.

Gradually my eyes adjusted to the gloom and each time the door opened the blast of sunlight across the bar was like beacon, briefly illuminating the bar rail denizens.

"Nice place," I said, the soul of wit. "Come here often?"

"No one knows us here. I wanted to see you someplace other than your apartment. It's just too depressing."

The door opened and the light swept along the bar. I couldn't help noticing a fellow who seemed to be watching us with great interest.

"I feel like you have something you wish to discuss with me, at a neutral site. I'm guessing here, but might it have something to do with your marital status?"

Even in the dark, I saw I'd scored a palpable hit.

"His name is John. We live together like brother and sister," she explained. "I caught him cheating, with his secretary. I suspected, and I went through his briefcase and found his American Express bill. There were room charges to the Holiday Inn in Sharonville. When I confronted him, he admitted it."

More the fool he. Deny, deny and deny. Even the rankest cheater knows that. And I wondered if charges for a pair of new suits would be on next month's AMEX bill.

The door opened again, and the fellow who'd shown such interest in Debby and me was no longer on his stool. He was boiling down the aisle, his eyes locked on Debby like a laser guided missile.

"Unless I miss my guess, Brother John has arrived."

"Ah ha!"

Can you believe it —a walking, talking cliché of a suburban couple?

"I knew you didn't get that rug burn at the gym."

And how did your brother get such a close look at your naked back? Oh Debby, for shame.

"You followed me!" She shrieked.

"I didn't have to. I tracked your smart phone GPS," Brother John retorted.

"That's an invasion of my privacy!"

Even in the gloom, Brother John had the look of a desk-bound drone, an accountant maybe, and I sensed dear Debby was in no physical danger. They had each other's full attention, perhaps for the first time in a long time.

And according to rule one, it was time to Go With the Flow. I took the occasion to rise and slip out the back

In a way I felt used —used to punish an errant husband— and maybe rescue a marriage. I keyed the ignition to my new Camaro and wondered if I'd missed my calling, that perhaps a career as a marriage doctor was my true North.

ABOUT
THE
AUTHORS

KIMBERLY ARMSTRONG

Kimberly Armstrong hails from Chicago. She is a poet, and also pretty good at writing essays –though she rarely gets around to that. She concerns herself with social science, inequality, humanism and Judaism. (5779 is her year!) She loves reading, singing, learning languages, and science fiction. She is well-traveled, and will visit her eighth foreign country in 2019. Who knows, maybe she will also finish one of those four shawls she's knitting that are all 96% done. Stranger things have happened.

JENNY BREEDEN

Jenny Breeden was born and raised in Erlanger, Kentucky, and moved to Covington in 1985. She has three grandchildren. She enjoys traveling, photography, scrapbooking, and crafts such as jewelry making, crocheting, cross-stitch, and painting. A Northern Kentucky University alum, Jenny is an avid reader and considers herself a lifelong learner. She's written poetry and short stories over the years, including mysteries, historical fiction and person narratives.

She joined the Covington Writers Group in 2014 and has been a driving force in getting their anthologies published each year. By sharing her knowledge and experience in the self-publishing world through workshops and seminars, she's helped others move forward with getting their dreams in print.

LESLIE BUSH

Leslie Bush has lived all her life in Covington, graduated from Holmes High School in '84 and NKU in '88 with a Bachelor's Degree in English. Her interest is in 19th Century British and French literature and Fantasy and Science Fiction.

She has been writing since she was 11, and she writes primarily in the Fantasy genre with a twisted sense of humor. She prides herself on her black humor. What can she say; she's a bloody goth. It is a world of magic and fiction. Anything is possible.

MIKEY CHLANDA

Mikey Chlanda is a full-time author after taking injury retirement from the fire department, ending his career as a lieutenant leading an engine crew. He has fourteen published books under his own name along with two pen names, with more on the way. He writes regularly for Huffington Post, Forbes.com, Seeking Alpha, Fire Engineering, Fire Nation and Medium. His work has also appeared in the New York Times, the Village Voice, Writers Weekly, Family Life, and many more. He has been featured speaker at the Kenton County Library, Cincinnati Digital Marketers, Indie Author Day 2017, We Put Stuff on the Web, Columbus Library, and the Louisville Library. His upcoming book "I Am D. B. Cooper" is available on pre-order through Amazon.

PATTI KAY EMERSON

Patti Kay Emerson was born in September 1960 in Covington, Kentucky, where she lived until she moved to Florence, Kentucky in 2015. She graduated from Gateway Community and Technical College in 2010 with a 3.4 GPA with an Associate in Art Degree. She was also inducted into Phi Theta Kappa, an international honor society for two-year colleges.

BARBARA HOWARD

Barbara Howard helped children and adults with special needs reach their greatest potential and an improved quality of life through 36 years of service to Redwood School & Rehabilitation Center, including one year as speech-language pathologist, 11 years as Director/Adult Services, and 24 years as Executive Director/CEO. These roles required many skill sets, including the ability to write grants and funding proposals, policy manuals, marketing materials, job descriptions, employment documents, and so on.

When Barbara retired in 2015, she did not want to lose the ability to write. Her daughter Aliena –a member of the Independence Inklings– encouraged her to join the group. Barbara learned that writing fiction is very different than technical writing. The flash fiction included in this anthology was her first piece of fiction. Currently, she is working on a fantasy novel and hopes to soon complete the first draft. Barbara also enjoys writing short stories, memoir, and poetry.

On days when she is not writing, Barbara can be found hiking, canoeing, kayaking, bicycling, or camping with her husband, Ben. She has three other daughters, Tracy Schwartz, Brenna Howard, and Barbara Bass. Everyone in the family provides an ear, helpful feedback, and encouragement to keep writing.

Brad Hudepohl

R. Brad Hudepohl grew up in the western part of Cincinnati He attended Western Hills High School. He has a Bachelor of Arts in German from The Ohio State University and a Bachelor of Science in Pharmacy from the University of Cincinnati. He had worked as a pharmacist since 1976 and is currently retired.

MIRSADA KADIRIC

Mirsada Kadiric was born in Bosnia and immigrated to the US as a refugee in 1998 when she was sixteen years old. Not speaking the English language, and unfamiliar with the American culture, Mirsada initially struggled to adjust. She found a way to flourish during her higher education years at Northern Kentucky University and was recognized as the Outstanding Student in Marketing (2004), the Outstanding Young Researcher of the Decade (2012), and Alumni Humanitarian of the Year (2018).

She is employed at Kao USA, Inc. in market research for the John Frieda brand. With the global refugee crisis unfolding in the news, Mirsada was moved to act and speak up for those who are facing the same struggles her and her family. She currently volunteers with a local nonprofit organization called RefugeeConnect.

On April 5th, 2018, Mirsada released her first book, titled "I Am a Refugee: Finding Home Again in America". The book is a memoir reflecting her personal refugee story. She wanted this book to serve as a voice for refugees around the world. In her free time, Mirsada loves to explore the world with her partner, checking off cities and countries on their long travel wish list.

ELLE MOTT

Elle Mott is an established writer in creative nonfiction and is published in literary journals, a national news magazine, and in anthologies local to greater Cincinnati, Ohio. Drawn from personal experience, Elle writes about homelessness, community concerns, spirituality, and humanitarianism. Recognized for her volunteering efforts, she received an award, "Community Service Leader of the Year, 2017" from an area non-profit organization.

Elle's debut book, "Out of Chaos: A Memoir" was released with Boyle & Dalton Publishers in August 2018. It is in paperback and e-book on Amazon, through Barnes & Noble, and other places world-wide. It is also available through Walmart e-books and other major e-book outlets.

Elle has called Northern Kentucky her home since May 2013. Her work as a library page is her livelihood while writing is her joy. She values her friendships, pet finches, and community of neighbors. Connect with Elle on Twitter @NovElle, on Facebook at ellemott.author/ and through her website and blog, http://ellemottauthor.com/

L. N. PASSMORE

As soon as she could walk, L. N. Passmore toddled into the sea. At age six she got lost in the woods, perfect for communing with tree spirits and departed ancestors. No wonder living in the Appalachians made forested mountains—filled with secret music and light—her muses. Her beloved cats, dogs, and horse became wise counselors.

She has lived, worked, and traveled all over USA, from Alaska and the Navajo Nation in Arizona to the Atlantic Coast; and the UK, from John o' Groats to Land's End. Her first of many extended trips to the Scottish Highlands brought her home to a land new to her eyes but not her soul. Visits to the western isles: Mull, Iona, Staffa, and Skye, where the veil between worlds is the thinnest, revealed the truth of Old Powers.

Passmore's *Wayward Wulves Beware*, Book 1 of the Eye of the Wulf Series, is for sale, hardcopy and e-book, at amazon.com and soon to be available at Barnes and Noble and other local bookstores. Visit her website, Moving Mountains at: www.lnpassmore.com to read her *Tales of Appalachia, Tales of Lisnafaer,* and her Blog: *Mountain Musings.*

GARY REED

Gary Reed is the author of the legal thriller <u>A Fatal Cell Phone Video</u> and the historical novel <u>Things Could Get Ugly</u>.

Gary Reed draws on his extensive legal experience in his writing. He practiced law in a large law firm and later in an in-house capacity. Throughout his career, he managed litigation and investigations across the country.

He has always been interested in writing. He wrote for and edited his high school and college newspapers and wrote professional articles in his areas of legal specialty.

Gary relies on a robust network of beta readers to make sure his works are easy to read and enjoyable. He is also an active participant in two writing groups.

D. P. SCHNUR

A retired insurance executive and former business writer, D. P. Schnur is a graduate of Miami University, Oxford, Ohio, As an inveterate classical humanist, he cleaves to the belief in the resilience of the human spirit. In addition to his many business, marketing and management articles, he has produced two collections of short stories: "Hitler Never Went to a Hunky Dance" and "The Wapanplop Song."

He and his wife Barbara divide their time between Florence, Kentucky and Michigan. After decades spent on the road, and quite a few transfers, it was a return to home ground in Kentucky fifteen years ago.

ALVENA STANFIELD

Alvena Stanfield is a published author of fiction and non-fiction stories. She has recently dabbled in teaching a multi-media experience in all genres and in screen writing. She attends Northern Kentucky University and is on the Scholars List. Her short story "Abolishing Solitary Confinement" can be found in "The Power of 'Yes,'" *Chicken Soup for the Soul,* published in August 2018.

Most recently her interests are historic fiction set in the mid-nineteenth century western frontier. She's still working on her novel Frontier Messenger, expected to be available through Amazon in 2019. To receive a pre-pub chapter, contact 859-409-3434 or stanfieldwrites@gmail.com.

JAN WERFF

Jan Werff is an old crank who barely skimmed his way through Northern Kentucky University. Upon graduation he slaved away in the employ of a number of fly-by-night outfits before finding his true north as a long-haul trucker. He is currently living the dream way out in the sticks with his wife, "Little Hitler," ten cats and two dogs.

CONTACT US

Connect with us at:

CovingtonWritersGroup@outlook.com

and

Facebook.com/CovingtonWritersGroup